DELAY OF GAME

PLAYING DIRTY

BOOK THREE

LANE HART

COPYRIGHT

This book is a work of fiction. The characters, incidents, and dialogue were created from the author's imagination and are not to be construed as real. Any resemblance to actual people or events is coincidental.

The author acknowledges the copyrighted and trademarked status of various products within this work of fiction.

Editor's Choice Publishing

P.O. Box 10024

Greensboro, NC 27404

Edited by Angela Snyder
Cover by Vanilla Lily Designs
https://www.vanillalilydesigns.com/

WARNING: THIS IS A M/M SWEET AND SEXY STORY THAT CONTAINS ADULT LANGUAGE AND EXPLICIT SEX SCENES.

For Christy W. and Jennifer L.

Thank you both so much for inspiring me to write this unexpected love story.

PROLOGUE

Lathan Savage

Four years earlier...

As soon as I step onto Kohen Hendricks' new yacht, the collar of my gray cotton tee begins tightening around my throat, threatening to choke me to death. The July humidity and my social awkwardness are making it incredibly difficult to get enough oxygen in my lungs. I tug on the front of my shirt to try and stretch it out as I squeeze through the crowd and slip into the interior of the boat seeking air conditioning. God, there are so many people here tonight and a ton of beautiful women, not that I would even know how to start talking to them.

Tonight's my first party as a professional football player but I'm way out of my league. On the inside, I'm still the shy, chubby boy who didn't have many friends in school. My love of football is the only thing that got me off the couch when I was a teenager. I idolized

Jerry Rice, Dan Marino, and Joe Montana. And maybe I thought that, if I worked hard enough, my peers would like me rather than make fun of me.

During high school, I was called "Pork Sausage," constantly ridiculed by the jocks I played football with and ignored by all the girls. At a party some of the senior players threw when I was sixteen, they locked me in a bedroom with Brooke Douglas, one of the biggest sluts in school. She was rumored to have slept with most of the team, even a few at the same time. While I didn't expect her to have sex with me that night, I thought maybe I would get lucky and have my first kiss. But then she looked at me in disgust and said, "They expect me to fuck you for a hundred bucks? Never gonna happen, Porky. Maybe if you lose about fifty pounds, I might reconsider..."

Needless to say, I didn't get my first kiss that night. No, that didn't happen until I was a sophomore in college. I was still overweight as an offensive linemen but in better shape since I was away from my mom's comfort food. Adrianne, a party girl from my chemistry class, started talking to me at a bar one night and asked to go back to my dorm. I snuck her in, but I should've known she had been drinking too much for what we planned to do. Instead, I found out the hard way.

Adrianne was my first kiss as soon as we sat down on my twin dorm bed. It was wet and sloppy, and I didn't really enjoy it at all. My dick finally started perking up when she knelt between my legs and unzipped my jeans. But just as she put my cock in her mouth, she gagged and threw up all over my lap.

I should probably mention here that I have a really weak stomach, so seeing *her* vomit made me vomit all over the top of her head. It was a disgusting mess that nearly got me kicked out of the dorms.

So, while I may have worked my ass off to lose weight and drastically improve my performance on the field as a tight end rather than a linebacker these past four years, I'm yet to make any real friends or lose my virginity.

It's way past time for me to finally take that last step into manhood. How hard can it be? If I was lucky enough to be one of the few college players to get drafted into the league, finding a woman to pop my cherry should be easy.

Tonight, there are plenty of women on Kohen's new yacht, if only I knew how to start talking to one without sounding like a bumbling idiot. Or worse, a twenty-one-year-old virgin.

Fuck, who am I kidding? My face is turning tomato red just thinking about introducing myself.

Across the room, a raven-haired beauty catches my eye and smiles. She's pretty. Definitely too pretty for me.

Since I'm standing in a room full of strangers, I find an empty spot on the wall to lean my back against and pull out my phone, making it look like I'm texting my non-existent friends rather than staring at the weather forecast.

"Hey, you're Lathan, right?"

I glance up and find the dark-haired woman I was staring at earlier standing right in front of me. Her breasts that are spilling out the top of her red dress look so damn succulent my mouth goes dry, wanting a taste. Wait, did she say my name?

"Ah, yeah, I'm Lathan," I reply, having to clear my throat when I straighten in surprise and pull my eyes back up to hers.

"Kohen told me you're new to the team this year and were a first-round draft pick," she says, offering me her palm to shake. "I'm Lola, one of the Lady Cats."

"Oh, well, um, nice to, ah, meet you," I manage to get out through the stammering.

Holy shit. I can't believe one of the cheerleaders knows my name and is actually talking to me.

"Will you dance with me?" she asks while batting her long, black eyelashes.

"Sorry, but I don't dance," I sadly admit.

"Oh, well, that's too bad," she replies with a fake pout, drawing my attention to her red, luscious lips. "Maybe we could find an empty bedroom, and I can just dance for you?"

Fuck, yes! This losing my virginity thing might be easier than I thought.

Wait, I probably need to tell her that out loud.

"Y-yeah. I mean, yes, let's do that," I agree.

Taking my hand, the woman whose name I don't even remember leads me down a short hallway and into a dark room. Once we're inside, she locks the door and flips on the overhead light, revealing a large bed.

"Get comfortable," she says, nodding to the mattress while her hands start tugging her short red dress up her thighs. "It's hard to move in this," she explains, and then it's up and over her head, revealing a tiny black thong and matching push-up bra.

I walk backward, taking in the sight before me until the back of my legs hit the bed and my ass goes down on the mattress. This is the first time I've ever seen a half-naked woman up close and personal rather than on my laptop screen. She's beautiful; there's no denying that, and yet I don't have any idea what the fuck I'm supposed to do.

The cheerleader does a few fancy leg kicks in the air and spins in the middle of the floor before she ends up on the bed with me, straddling my lap and kissing me. Not sure where I should put my hands, I just keep them planted on the mattress on either side of me.

"You can touch me," she says against my lips. Picking up one of my hands, she places it on her ass and then positions the other over one of her breasts. That's the point at which I completely freeze up.

She feels good, looks amazing, and smells delicious like cinnamon, but something's just not...right. I don't even remember her name, Layla or Laura maybe, and I have no clue what the fuck I'm doing.

Breaking the kiss, I lift the woman from my lap by her narrow waist and place her on the bed beside me so that I can get to my feet.

"Sorry," I tell her as my cheeks and the back of my neck blaze hot.

"Aww, what's wrong?" she asks while I pick up her dress from the floor and hand it back to her. "Do you have a girlfriend?"

"Yes, a girlfriend," I lie as my excuse for freaking out before I begin backing out of the room.

"No one has to know. I won't tell if you don't," she says to me while running her hand between her legs.

"Ah, n-nice to meet you. Sorry, again," I tell her before I make my escape from the room.

This was all too much too soon. It was stupid to think I could go from virgin to Casanova during one fucking party. I've waited too long, and now sex is all built up to this monumental thing in my head. Women my age are all experienced by now, especially that cheerleader, so I'm bound to be one hell of a disappointment to them in the sack. That's not how I want my first time to be, a complete and utter embarrassment that I'll never rebound from. I need to find a girl I like and take things slow, build up to reaching the end zone one play at a time instead of rushing down the field and fumbling.

Just as I'm about to make my escape out the yacht's interior exit to avoid any more awkward encounters, I run into Kohen Hendricks.

"Hey, it's Lathan, right? Our new tight end. Have you met Cameron and Nixon yet?" he asks, placing a hand on my shoulder to stop me.

"Uh, no, I don't think so," I say, turning around and plastering a smile on my face since it would be rude to ignore my new teammates. Holding out my hand, I first shake with the one with tattoos and then the other with shoulder length blond hair.

"You're the tight end from Georgia State, aren't you?" the blond guys asks.

"Yep, that's me," I answer.

"Everyone's been talking about that play from the Orange Bowl when you had, like, five dudes hanging off of you and you still made it fifteen yards into the end zone!" the tattooed teammate says.

"I got lucky," I reply shyly with a shrug while slipping my hands into my jean pockets.

"Bullshit! You're built like a tank," the blond declares.

"Unfortunately," I agree.

"You need a beer in your hand," Kohen says. "Let's remedy that."

Not wanting to pussy out and tell them I was trying to get out of dodge before the hot cheerleader I embarrassed myself in front of finds me, I follow the guys back into the kitchen. That's where Cameron and Nixon bet a hundred bucks on who can drink the most beers in five minutes and I continue to sip on my first bottle. These guys are actually funny and nice, nothing like the hateful dickheads I played with in high school or college. Although, I guess it helps that I'm no longer three hundred blubbery pounds.

"Evening, gentlemen," Quinton Dunn, the team's new quarterback, says when he joins us with a crooked smile on his handsome face. "You'll never believe the things one of the Lady Cats just did to me."

"Nice!" Cameron tells him. He hands Quinton a beer from the fridge and then clangs his bottle to it in cheers. "Let's hear it!"

"All right, so I walked out of the bathroom, and bam! She just threw herself at me. Next thing I know we're in a bedroom and sixty-nining...while standing up!"

"Whatever," one of the guys remarks.

"I'm serious!" Quinton declares. "Then she did this upside down split thing in the air and told me to fuck her like that..."

"Wait...what was the girl's name?" Kohen suddenly asks.

"Ah, shit, what was it?" Quinton mutters to himself. "Started with an L...Lena, Lona? Black hair. Ooh, I remember! It was Lola."

That's the last word Quinton speaks before Kohen's fist nails him smack dab on his smug mouth. All hell breaks loose on the boat after that.

"That's my fiancée...you stupid...motherfucker!" Kohen shouts while his fists continue beating on Quinton's face, and Quinton begins to retaliate.

Holy shit! Lola is with Kohen? And she cheated on him with Quinton?

While I'm helping my new teammates try to separate the two guys to keep them from killing each other, I realize that it could've been *me* getting the beatdown if I hadn't put on the brakes and walked away from that girl.

Women aren't worth all this trouble, that's for damn sure.

I may be desperate to lose my virginity, but it just doesn't seem worth the headache.

So, right then and there between flying fists, I decided that someday I'll find a nice, quiet girl that my parents will love, and I'll want to marry. Then, and only then, will I sleep with her.

CHAPTER 1

Paxton Price

Present day...

"Come on, Pax. I miss you and I need you so much," Oliver whines through the phone at my ear, sounding like a crack addict. More like cock addict.

"Shouldn't you be saying those things to your *wife*?" I ask as I get up from the computer to stretch my legs.

"You know she can't give me what I need. Only you can."

"Then come out of the fucking closet already!" I yell at him in frustration, jerking on a handful of my auburn hair. And, fuck, I hate messing my hair up, but that's the effect Oliver has on me. The two of us fucked probably a dozen times before he finally owned up to being a married man. That was about two months ago, and I've refused to see him ever since.

"I am. I will come out. Charlotte and I are over. We've separated."

Maybe I'm a fucking fool, but I want to believe him this time, even though I know better.

"That's what you said the last time," I remind him of a few weeks ago when I insisted that if he and his wife were over that I would just come over to his place. He backpedaled real fast after that to keep me from meeting his wife.

"I'm serious this time," Oliver says. "We're getting a divorce! I'll... I'll show you the paperwork."

If he has paperwork, then he's started the process. Could he actually be serious about ending his marriage for me?

"I've already signed it at my attorney's office; I just need to get her signature," he adds when I remain silent.

"Fine. But you better not be lying to me, or we're done. I mean it, Ollie."

"Okay, I am. I promise," he agrees halfheartedly. "I'm leaving work and on my way to your place."

"See you then," I tell him with a sigh.

I always seem to find myself in these situations with men who are bisexual. They enjoy being with me when it suits them but usually end up going back to women because it's easier to be heterosexual. No one bats an eye if they take a woman on a date or kiss her in public. I'm usually their dirty little secret, hidden from the rest of the world because they don't want to deal with the public opinion of two men being together.

Fifteen minutes later, there's a knock on my door. Part of me wants to ignore him but the other is so desperate for the intimacy I've missed that I can't open the door fast enough.

I pull it open and find Oliver in the remnants of his work clothes. He looks ruffled yet just as hot, an accountant hiding the body of Adonis underneath his suit. I grab the front of Oliver's dress shirt, making his chocolate eyes widen in surprise before I slam the door closed and kiss him. His dick is already hard against mine and begging for a release; but since he fucked me over the last time we did this, he's going to have to earn his orgasm.

Pulling back, I let go of his shirt and tell him, "Get on your knees."

He does so without hesitation, undoing my pants the next second with practiced fingers. As soon as my cock is free, he takes me deep into his mouth causing me to groan from the pleasure. "That's right. Get it nice and wet before I fuck you with it."

Some gay guys top and some bottom, several even switch hit, but Paxton Price doesn't bottom for anyone. I do all the fucking.

And Oliver isn't the only married man who's asked me to rail him either. You would be surprised how many bisexual men are out there, able and willing to fuck a woman but secretly wanting to get fucked by men. So, while they may perform just fine for their girlfriend and wives in the bedroom, every once in a while, they crave what only I can give them --- a good hard fuck that makes them blow their load faster than you can snap your fingers.

Those hair-trigger ones are always the same. Their instinctual urges suppressed for so long that I barely touch them and they explode. After that, they're usually content to toss me aside and go back to their "normal" lives to pretend they're heterosexual for a while.

I'm done with being the mistress or having to sneak around. Either Ollie's serious about us being an actual couple and he'll stay tonight to prove it, or I'm done. But first, he owes me an orgasm.

A repetitive, rhythmic buzzing distracts me from the attempt to stay in the moment. Buzzing that's coming from Oliver's pants pocket.

"That's enough," I tell him, ending his enthusiastic blow job before I finish when I lose my release. "Get naked and bend over the sofa," I tell him, pulling him up from the floor by the top of his blond hair.

"Let me...I'll go get undressed in the bathroom," he says before disappearing down the hall.

On my way to the bedroom to get the condoms and lube, I linger by the bathroom door and listen to Oliver's telephone conversation.

"No, no! You don't need to bring me dinner. I'm wrapping up a few emails, and then I'll be on my way home. Okay, see you soon. Love you."

I fucking knew it!

Oliver was obviously talking to his wife on the phone. That son of a bitch isn't getting divorced, and he sure as shit isn't separated either!

Leaning my back directly across from the bathroom door, I cross my arms over my chest and wait for him to come out.

When the door opens, there stands Oliver in all his naked glory, the sleek, muscular body of a top athlete. Too bad his good looks have blinded me for so long that I couldn't see that this was never going to be more than an occasional fling to him.

"Get out," I tell him.

"What? Why?" he asks, blinking his brown eyes at me innocently.

"Who were you talking to on the phone?"

"My...sister," he looks at me and lies right to my face.

"Get the fuck out. And if you ever call me or come by here again, I'll tell your wife everything," I threaten.

Oliver opens his mouth to protest or play the divorce card but then thinks better of it. I watch as he slowly dresses again and then slinks away, out the door and out of my life for good.

Why do I keep letting assholes like Ollie use me? Probably because I'm a healthy man in my twenties and I like to have sex with other guys. When I was a teenager, I tried to be with a girl, to convince myself that jerking off to men's boxers ads was a fluke. I kept my cool while I removed her shirt and squeezed her tits; but when she grabbed my limp dick, I wanted to push her away rather than ask her to keep going.

That was the end of my exploring with the opposite sex. I can appreciate the beauty of women, like my gorgeous best friend Roxy, but that's the extent of it.

I'm gay, always have been and always will be, and I won't hide that for anyone.

CHAPTER 2

Lathan

After today's win against the Miami Mariners, my teammates and I shake hands with the players on the visiting team, and then most of them rush back to the locker room. They're excited to shower and get changed to see their family, to go out and celebrate.

Like every game this season, there's no one here for me today.

My mom is too weak to travel; the cancer is eating away at her a little more each day. And there's no way my dad will leave her side even if someone else could stay with her. I get it; he wants to spend every single minute with her that he can before she...

While Elon is only a three-hour drive west from Wilmington, between practices I can't miss any away games, I don't get to visit my parents as much as I would like to. Knowing how fragile my mother is and that her days are limited makes me consider throwing away my professional football career that I worked so hard for, just to be with her these last days.

I fucking hate that all the money in my bank account isn't worth a shit because she's tried surgeries, radiation, chemo, and none of them have worked. Her cancer just keeps manifesting in more organs. It started in her kidneys, then went into her liver, and now it's taking over her pancreas.

The lack of control I have over her illness has me constantly angry and frustrated nowadays. I want to hit something or...or eat something. Comfort food like fried chicken and greasy triple cheese and meat pizza have always been my downfall. Instead of going out with the guys tonight, maybe I'll go back to my townhouse and pig out instead. It won't be like before when I was three-hundred pounds; just one day of indulging and then hours of training tomorrow.

I seriously need to find a way to burn off all this stress and constant worry. Due to the league's contract restrictions, I can't take up boxing, MMA, or any other sport where I could get hurt. So that leaves running, weight lifting, and binge eating.

Before my mom got sick, I could relieve some stress with masturbation. Now, the sexual frustration just constantly builds inside me without an outlet because I can't even get a decent hard-on lately. My limp dick and I are fucking pathetic.

I've given up on losing my virginity. Instead of getting all worked up about asking a girl out, I don't even bother anymore. I know how it will end, with me fumbling around like an idiot and crashing and burning. It's not worth the effort.

Soaking my banged up right knee in the training center's jacuzzi, I decide that tonight after I go home and pig out, I'll put on some porn to try and get aroused enough to ease the pent-up aggression. My X-rated movie collection isn't huge, just a few hot videos with big breasted women getting their brains fucked out by men who are well hung with nice, smooth physiques. I usually fast-forward through the blowjobs.

Till this day I can't forget my one miserably failed attempt in college or watch the act without my stomach rolling. Call me crazy, but vomit on my dick is not much of an aphrodisiac. I'll stick to the doggy style porno scenes, thank you very much.

Able to bend and straighten my leg in the warm water without groaning in pain, I finally climb out and head for the shower where I quickly scrub my head with shampoo and wash my body.

By the time I get to the locker room, Cameron, my last teammate, is leaving. With a quick goodbye, he hurries out to reunite with his friends or family. I probably should get a move on too so I can call and check in with my parents...

"Whoa! Holy washboard abs, Batman!"

I startle at the sudden, echoing comment in the otherwise empty, silent locker room. Reflexively, I reach down to grasp the towel tighter around my waist to hold it in place while seeking out the voice coming from the doorway to my right.

Instantly recognizing the handsome, auburn-haired man in an immaculate suit, I blow out a breath of relief that it's not some crazy stalker fan.

Actually, I shouldn't relax just yet...

"What the hell are you doing in here, Pax?" I ask the gay best friend of Roxy, our team and the league's only female player. "By now you know damn well that Roxy's locker room is on the other side of the stadium."

Wait, did I mentally call him *handsome*?

And was he complimenting my abs when he walked in?

Glancing down, I realize my six-pack is pretty damn impressive thanks to the grueling game we just won and hours of dehydration. I should take a pic before I eat everything in sight and it reverts to a regular gut.

"I'm horrible with directions and shit," Pax replies, his voice growing louder as he steps further into the room.

Turning my back to him to dig in my duffle for a shirt, I gruffly tell him, "Yeah, well, get the fuck out. This isn't your personal peep show." I'm not entirely sure why I feel so defensive about his presence when I'm trying to get dressed.

"Go ahead and change, it's not like I've never seen a dick before," Pax replies, and I hear a metallic clang like he just rested his shoulder or back against a locker, intending to stick around. I refuse to look over at him to confirm.

"The problem is that you actually *like* looking at other dicks," I argue.

"That's not true," Pax says. "I like looking at my own dick too. It's a rather impressive unit in length and girth, but maybe I'm biased. I could show you and you could decide for yourself."

"Get the fuck out," I tell him when my cock gives an involuntary twitch at his arrogance. And while it's surprising, I tell myself to ignore it. It's probably just the hot water from jacuzzi tub heating up my blood, along with the thoughts of the porn I'm planning to watch when I get home.

"Ah, come on, Lathan. Don't be shy. Drop the towel and let me just see if your cock is as big as I think it is, and then I'll leave," Pax says, his request causing my pulse to race until all I can hear is the roaring sound of it in my ears. Shit, can he hear my heart pounding from ten feet away or see the partial tenting under my towel? My cock is obviously just happy to have any compliments or attention on it, even if it's from another man. A gay man who makes no excuses for his sexuality.

"One of these days you're gonna walk in on the wrong person and get your ass kicked," I warn him.

"Maybe, but you would be surprised by how many homos in hiding you'll find in any given locker room," he replies while I grab my t-shirt out of my duffle and pull it over my head. "In my experience, they're usually the last to leave, either because they doddle and take their time to get a good look at naked teammates, *or* they intentionally wait until everyone's gone to shower to change so that they won't give in to the temptation to look."

"What the fuck are you implying?" I snap at him when I spin around to face him again. "I have to soak my knee in the Jacuzzi for half an hour before I shower, so everyone's gone by the time I get done."

"That was a rather quick explanation you made there. And I'm pretty sure I'm picking up a hint of defensiveness," Pax says before his eyes lower to the front of my towel that's not covered by my shirt.

"I'm not gay," I declare, slapping my palm over it.

"Didn't say you were," Pax replies before he finally turns to leave. "But I don't think you're one hundred percent straight either judging by that stiffy you're sporting."

Arrogant asshole!

I hope he flies back to Tennessee or wherever the hell he's from soon and stays there, because I don't think I can stand another round of his bullshit.

With a quick glance to make sure he's really gone, I pull my boxer briefs on and then my jeans. My cell phone dings from within my duffle with a text message, and I don't need to look at it to know it's my dad.

Pax and his bullshit forgotten, I sit down on one of the benches to get my socks and shoes on. Then, with my phone in one hand, I grab my duffle ready to leave.

When I step out of the stadium into the parking lot, I hit send to call my parents' home phone.

"Hey! Great game today, son!" my dad answers.

"Thanks," I tell him with a smile on my face.

"Wish we could've been there," he says.

"I know, me too, but you need to be there," I reply. "How's Mom?"

His sigh is all the answer I need. "She's not having a good day. I don't think she's been awake more than ten minutes here and there."

Reaching my white Jeep Wrangler, I unlock the door and throw my duffle into the passenger seat with more force than is required.

"Have you talked to the doctor?" I ask him as I climb inside and shut the driver door. "Is there something they can give her for more energy?"

"No, it's just a side effect of the recent chemo," he answers. "That's why Mom said she's done."

"What?" I exclaim. "Done with what?"

"The chemo. She doesn't –"

"She can't just stop the chemo!" I shout through the phone. "If she does...the doctor said weeks, at most."

"It's her decision, son, not mine or yours," my dad argues. "Do you think I agree with her decision?"

"Fuck," I mutter, slamming my left hand against the steering wheel. "Let me talk to her. Maybe I can change her mind."

Exhaling heavily, he says, "You can try when you come home for Thanksgiving. But honestly, I don't think it will do any good. It'll just upset you and her both."

Goddamn it! Stupid fucking cancer. There are cures for almost everything in the world except for the one thing killing my mom.

"She's sleeping now, but I can have her call you when she wakes up," Dad says.

My throat is so scratchy I have to clear it before I can speak one word. "Okay."

"Love you, son. Talk to you soon."

"Love you, too," I say quickly before ending the call.

Throwing my head back against the cushioned headrest, tears leak from the corners of my eyes as I send up a prayer to anyone who is listening to not take her from us so soon. She's the kindest, sweetest, most generous woman in the world, and she doesn't deserve this fate.

CHAPTER 3

Pax

When I was sixteen, right after the heterosexual experiment that I epically failed, I began to realize that no matter how much I tried, I wasn't attracted to women. Nothing got me harder than thick biceps, scruffy facial hair, a tight ass and a nice, big dick. That's when I decided to come out to my parents, to give up the charade and tell the world I was gay so that I could finally find one of those men to fuck.

I had no idea my dear old mom and dad would erupt with the heat and intensity of Old Faithful. First, they tried telling me I was wrong and that I was not attracted to men. Then, they blamed television for idealizing homosexuals, my Yankee school for being too liberal, my peers for lacking morals, and finally themselves for failing to raise a "normal" straight son.

So, I was shipped from New York to Tennessee where I lived with my grandmother and finished my last two years of high school.

Nana couldn't care less if I preferred sausage or tacos. So, from day one at my new school, I didn't hide my sexual preferences. Sure, I was called names, pushed around, some would say bullied, but all of that was worth it because I was finally having sex!

Being out, I attracted all of the closet gays within a thirty-mile radius. It didn't take long before I became more experienced than all my clandestine hookups. At the time, I wasn't upset that the guys I was seeing wanted to sneak around. They sucked my dick and let me fuck them, so it was all worth it. Or so I thought.

In college, the social scene was pretty much the same. Plenty of guys in the closet wanted to screw around, but few would actually agree to be seen in public with me for fear of being labeled gay. The jocks were the worst, always paranoid about teammates finding out. They didn't have to worry. I kept my mouth shut, enjoyed the sex, and then wasn't at all surprised when I didn't hear from them again.

Now, I'm twenty-seven, and I'm tired of being pulled back in the goddamn closet just to get laid!

The problem is I have a certain type --- hot, large, athletic, and preferably blond. I don't care for the weak, feminine bottoms that wear skinny jeans and weigh a buck twenty, if that. If I wanted a girl, I wouldn't be gay, would I? Unfortunately, for me, the type of men I like aren't usually big fans of being out and in the open, like Oliver. The more masculine they are, the more society says they shouldn't like cock.

For once in my life, is it too much to ask to find a nice, built man who isn't ashamed to hold my hand in public, go to dinner alone with me, or sweetly kiss me goodnight on my stoop?

It's exhausting to keep going through the same scenario with dates over and over again.

Maybe it's time for a change of scenery.

During college, I was the social butterfly, always hosting big ass parties and charging a fat admission to pay for my planning and throwing an epic event. Between that and the incredibly generous allowance my wealthy grandmother still insists on giving me, I've been saving and finally have enough money to start building my dream. I want to open a gay nightclub, a place where men can be themselves without worry of being ridiculed.

Now, I just have to decide where I should open up shop. Doing so here in Tennessee, where I've lived for the past six years, just doesn't seem like the optimal social environment. I need some place more...exciting, with great weather for an outdoor cabana, maybe even a swimming pool...

My cell phone rings as if on cue from my best friend Roxy, who recently moved to Wilmington to become the kicker for the Wildcats, their professional football team. I try to make it to all of her home games because I really like being there for her, and now with Roxy's crazy schedule, it's the only time I get to see her.

"How do you like living in Wilmington?" I ask her when I answer instead of a greeting.

Laughing, Roxy says, "Hello to you too, Pax!"

"Well?" I prompt.

"How do I feel about living in Wilmington?" she repeats.

"Yeah, do you like it down there? Are the people friendly, welcoming? Too conservative? Whenever I'm there for your games, it's only for like a day, so I need your take on it."

"The people in this area are great, and the beaches are so beautiful. I miss you, but I like it here," she replies. "If Kohen or I ever get traded, it will suck balls when we have to move."

"Nice," I tell her. "I was just trying to decide where to open up a nightclub..."

"Leave Tennessee and come here!" she exclaims excitedly into my ear. "You can stay with Kohen and me until you find your own place. I would freaking love to have you in my city again!"

"Then maybe I'll plan an extended trip soon," I agree, liking the idea of Wilmington more and more, not to mention all the hot football players in the area, including one tight end in particular who was throwing wood in the locker room.

"Great! I'll let Kohen know, but I'm sure he won't mind you staying here."

"I can get a hotel room, Roxy. It's no big deal," I assure her.

"Why would you do that when we have spare rooms?" she asks.

"Fine, I'll stay with you," I agree since it would be nice to save money. "So what's up? Just calling to check in?"

"Oh, right! We're playing the Tennessee Lightning this Sunday afternoon if you want to come? We'll be in town until Monday, so several of us will probably go out to dinner Sunday night."

"Several of you whom?" I ask.

"Um, you know, me, Kohen, Quinton, Callie, Lathan –"

"Count me in," I say since she just gave me all the reason I need to drive three hours across the state. An idea already forming, even if it is a terrible one, I tell her, "Text me your hotel info so I can try to get a room at the same place."

"Sure! I'm so glad you can make it. Dad can't, so it will be nice to have someone in the stands cheering for me."

"Number one cheerleader right here," I tell her with a grin. "Have a good week at practice, and I'll see you Sunday."

"You too! Love you, Pax."

"Love you too, Roxy," I say before hanging up.

Now, I just need to put my computer skills to the test and find a certain player's home address, and then I'll start scoping out properties in the area for my club.

Lathan can deny it all he wants; but if he's not gay or bisexual, then I'll suck my own dick. The man got hard just talking to me in the locker room! He was turned on because I asked to see his dick. Fuck, I know it's a bad idea, but I do love a challenge, and climbing in the closet with him for just one night would be worth the pain of being cast aside afterward. Lathan could be my last tryst before I give up pursuing men who don't want to be out for good. I'll seduce him to the dark side and then move on. He can try to resist, but I bet he's denied his urges for so long that he'll cave quicker than most.

And maybe, just maybe, it'll be good enough to make him come back for more.

CHAPTER 4

Lathan

After a grueling practice Wednesday, I park my Jeep in front of my townhouse and shuffle on achingly sore legs up the sidewalk. Fuck, I should've soaked my knee before leaving, but all I wanted to do was come home and fall into bed. My injury is directly related to the years I was gigantic and put too much stress on it, so I have no one but my formerly fat ass to blame.

When I'm a few feet away from my front door, I spot an obstruction on the welcome mat. One with a big red bow on top.

What the...

Getting closer, I see the bright yellow bananas inside the cellophane and realize it's a gift basket. Someone obviously made a mistake. It's probably for one of my neighbors, and the delivery company was in such a hurry that they just dropped it off at the first door they came to.

Finding the folded tag, I open it up to see who I need to get this sweet gift to. My eyes nearly pop out of my head when I see that the two neatly typed words are my name. It's addressed to me, but there's no sender information.

Who the hell would have a fruit basket delivered to me?

I do have some crazy but sweet fans out there, so I pick up the basket and rest it on my hip while I unlock the front door.

As soon as I'm inside, I sit down on my black leather sofa and untie the bow to dig in. I'm starving, and I'm hoping that there will be something inside to tell me who the damn thing is from.

I pull the plastic down to get to the goods; but just as I reach for the banana, I see the "real" gift.

A DVD.

Not just any DVD. The title of this one is *Curious,* and on the cover are two mostly naked dudes, one with his hand down the front of the other's pants.

What. The. Fuck?

Who the hell would...

Paxton!

Did that asshole send me gay porn? Why would he fucking do that?

I grab the card up from where I tossed it down next to me and open it again, trying to figure out the sender. Not seeing one, but just the address, phone number, and name of the delivery company, I pull my phone from my pocket and call it.

"Thank you for calling *Deliveries by Ellyn.* Can I help you?" a polite woman answers.

"Yeah, I had someone deliver a basket to my house, and I want to know who sent it!" I tell her.

"Oh, well, I'm sorry. Is there a problem with the basket?" she asks in concern.

"Yes. No. I mean, I just want to know who sent it. Please."

"Your name?"

"Lathan Savage."

"Oh, right. I remember that one," she says ominously. Yes, who *could* forget placing gay porn in the center of a fucking fruit basket?

A fruit basket.

Ha-ha. That asshole thinks he's so fucking funny. I am gonna punch the smirk off his handsome face the next time I see it. What if this woman tells someone about this and starts a rumor that I'm gay?

Ah! And why do I keep referring to him as handsome?

"Sir, the sender asked to remain anonymous," the lady on the phone tells me.

"Of course he did. Can't you tell me anything about him?"

"His billing address is in Tennessee, if that helps," she offers.

"Yep, that's all I needed to know," I tell her. "Thanks."

Ending the call, I pick up the damn DVD with two fingers on the corner edge like it may burn or bite me and carry it over to the trash can to toss it. I should throw away the whole damn basket but fuck it, I'm hungry, and it's healthy food to stuff my face with rather than *Twinkies*.

Sitting back down in front of the fruit, I dig into an apple, then peel and eat an orange. Finally, I make it back to the banana. Just as I start peeling the skin, it occurs to me how phallic this particular fruit is. I can even feel my cheeks burning when I stick the tip into my mouth and take a bite.

That motherfucker! How dare he find a way to make me blush while eating fruit in the privacy of my own damn house! He's gonna pay for this.

Gathering up my trash when I finish, I set the basket with the remaining fruit on the kitchen counter and toss the apple core, banana and orange peeling into the trash. Right on top of the picture of two men advertising sex. With each other.

There's no way I would ever watch that sort of porn. I like to see a woman's tits bounce as she gets fucked, especially when she's on top...

Surprisingly, my cock perks up right away at the thought. Rather than chance it deflating, I wake up the laptop in my bedroom with the disc already inside and start undressing as I hit play to pick up where I last stopped.

The woman's loud moans fill the otherwise silent room, followed by the man's occasional grunts as he pulls his cock all the way out of her pussy and then slams into her ass from behind. She seems to like that too based on the noises she's making, urging the man with a big dick to fuck her harder.

When I'm naked, I stretch out on the bed, lying on my side and start tugging on my cock from root to tip. I keep this up the entire time the two people on the screen are going at it, up and until he pulls his dick out of her and she gets on her knees to finish him off with her mouth.

Ugh. Why do they always have to end that way? And doesn't she know where that dick's just been?

Slamming the lid of the laptop down, I try to close my eyes and get myself off, but it's useless. I can't stop thinking about that fucking picture on the DVD in the trash. It's blocking my release.

I tug on my dick until it's raw with no luck, still so hard my balls may explode, and I can't do anything about it.

Hand lotion. That's what I need.

Rolling off the bed, I go to the master bathroom to search for some type of lube, but the bottle is empty. Just my luck.

So, I decide to take a nice hot shower, and use body wash to jerk off. I turn on the water and let it warm up a minute before climbing inside. The water and suds I squirt on my dick feel much better than doing it dry, but every time I close my eyes I see the blond man's bare ass with his hand down the auburn-haired guy's black athletic shorts. The damn image is even getting more specific in my head, and that's not helping my situation down below.

After rinsing off, I get out of the shower with my cock leading the way, dry off and then crash back out on my bed.

There has to be something I can do to ease the ache...

Nu-uh. Nope. Not gonna happen.

There's no way that will work if nothing else will, right?

Thinking about it, no one would know if I watched the DVD. I'll tell Pax I threw it in the trash when I confront that bastard. And I *will* throw it away again, just as soon as I watch it because I'm desperate and...curious. How *do* two men do it?

Besides, I bet it'll be so gross that I can't even finish one scene.

Jumping to my feet, I retrieve the DVD from underneath the discarded fruit, tear off the plastic wrap, and pop it into the laptop.

The scene begins with two young, buff, twenty-somethings in an outdoor hot tub, talking about what a great run they had together. The blond one says he needs a shower to cool off, and the auburn-haired one says that sounds like a good idea.

While the blond guy takes off his shorts and starts washing in a see-through stand-up shower, the other man gets undressed and watches. After several moments, the guy in the shower starts soaping up his dick, which turns into him jerking it, sort of like I was just doing. The other guy asks if he needs a hand, and Blondie tells him sure.

Auburn-haired guy steps into the shower and grabs the dude's dick, making him throw his head back and moan. They play with each other's swords for a while until the auburn guy goes down to his knees and starts sucking off the blond guy. Normally, this is the point at which I have to end the movie, memories of vomit in long brown hair and all over my junk too much to bear. Not this time. The camera does a close up of the guy on his knees with his mouth full as he takes every inch without gagging. In fact, he looks like he's enjoying looking up at Blondie's face to see his reaction, which is...euphoric. Lips parted, eyes closed tight, he looks like he's about to...

"Fuck!" I exclaim as my release slams into me unexpectedly. My balls draw up tight as my body clenches and my cock spews like a never-ending geyser. The instant, featherlike drifting sensation of bliss is a welcome reprieve from my constant state of dread. I close my eyes and soak it up while it lasts until the grunts and groans on my computer bring me back to my bedroom. That's when I remember I'm watching gay porn. The guilt and confusion hit me harder than a ton of bricks.

I try to convince myself that no one will ever know I got off to one man giving another a blowjob, but the problem is I know the truth.

And I sure as fuck won't be able to forget it.

CHAPTER 5

Pax

By the start of the fourth quarter of Sunday's game, it's clear to everyone in the stadium that the Wildcats are going to lose. They're down by twenty-one points, and not even their star quarterback can save them.

The loss can't be pinned on one particular player. No, the whole game has been a clusterfuck of fumbles, sacks, interceptions, and just overall poor performance.

It's a shame the offense has been so awful. That means I've hardly had a chance to ogle Lathan Savage before the Tennessee Lightning's defense makes them go three and out, forcing them off the field. From what I have seen of him on the sidelines when he removes his helmet, he looks frustrated.

Good thing I know just how to cheer him up.

The delivery company confirmed that he received his gift basket, so all week I've been wondering the same thing --- was Lathan curious enough to watch it? Even if he did, I doubt someone as macho as the tight end would admit it.

Tonight, at dinner, I'll ask him. And he'll either laugh it off good-naturedly or flip out. If he flips out, then I'll assume he's upset at himself for caving.

Honestly, I know how stupid this crush of mine is, and that it is going to end badly, yet I can't make myself back off. Lathan Savage is not gay; of that, I'm almost certain. What I'm desperate to find out is if he's a closet bisexual. If he is, I want to be the first man to fuck him.

...

Lathan

It feels like I'm on a date. A date with a fucking dude.

Everyone at the restaurant table is paired up, each couple sitting across from each other, Quinton and Callie, Roxy and Kohen. And then there's me and...Paxton.

Yep, doesn't look like I'm capable of escaping that bastard.

And he obviously knows his presence bothers me, because the stupid smirk on his face hasn't slipped once.

"So, Lathan, what are you getting tonight?" Pax asks while reading over the menu. "Tossed salad, or a big slab of meat? The sausage stuffed rigatoni looks good too."

Ugh, I'm not usually one to drink, but it's gonna take a lot more alcohol to get through this meal if he keeps up the sexual innuendos the entire time.

"Can I get another Jager?" I ask the waiter when he passes by our table, holding up the glass I just drained.

"Sure thing," the college kid replies with a wink, nearly making me groan in annoyance, especially when I hear Pax's chuckle.

"And keep them coming," I shout to the waiter's retreating back.

"Any particular reason you're planning on getting shitfaced?" Pax asks me with one pretentious eyebrow arched.

"In case you didn't notice, we lost badly today," I grumble. "And why do you care?"

"I don't," he replies while reaching down to straighten his tie.

"What's with you and the suits?" I ask since he always seems to be wearing one. Not that I notice his attire, the fancy clothes just always stand out. "Do you moonlight as a sleazy used car salesman or something?"

"I like to look nice," he answers. "And no, I'm not a used car salesman, I'm a highly-paid gigolo."

"I'm sorry, you're a *what*?"

"Male prostitute. I fuck men for money," Pax responds without even blinking.

Glancing at the two couples sitting with us, I check to see if they heard him, but they're too engrossed by gazing into each other's eyes or whatever the fuck that couples apparently do that they didn't seem to hear.

"You're lying," I tell him, convinced he's screwing with me. He enjoys trying to get a rise out of me, which is why he sent that damn fruit basket.

"If you say so," is his unconcerned response. His eyes stay lowered to the menu in front of him. "I think I'm gonna get the salmon."

"Whatever," I reply on a sigh.

"So, you didn't contra*dict* me last week," Pax says when he closes his menu and looks up, nailing me with his dark eyes. "Do empty locker rooms get you excited or was that because of...something else?"

"I don't know what the fuck you're talking about," I tell him through clenched teeth, looking around for the waiter with my second round.

"Hey, don't get pissy. Your secret's safe with me," Pax says with a grin and a wink.

"What secret? There *is* no secret," I lean across the table to hiss at him.

"Then why are you whispering?" he asks, lowering his own voice. "I'm not gonna tell a soul that you watched gay porn...and liked it. I am *curious,* though..." he says, emphasizing the title of the DVD that I watched in its entirety before I threw it in the garbage. And ever since Wednesday night, I've been having these weird dreams and waking up hot and sweaty with my dick in my hand or humping the mattress. I think I might be losing my mind.

"So, tell me, *tight end,*" Pax starts, licking his lips intentionally when he knows I'm looking at him. "When you were watching, did you fantasize about being the one getting plowed or the one doing the plowing?"

"Shut the fuck up!" I snap so loudly that now the group turns and looks at me, along with half the restaurant, which is bad since plenty of people recognize me and my teammates in public.

Pax's question just hit a nerve because in my dreams I'm the one in control, pounding into a faceless woman. Okay, so maybe it was a man who was bent over or on all fours. Except for that one time...

And great, now my dick has decided to get hard at the absolute worst time.

"Here you go, sir," the waiter says when he starts to sit down my drink. I intercept it from his hand and drain it instead. To survive tonight, I need to be drunk.

When I'm finished, I offer the waiter the glass back. "I'll be right back with another," he tells me. "Is everyone ready to order?"

"I don't think Lathan knows what he wants yet," Pax speaks up and says with a grin.

"Oh, I know what I want. I want breasts!" I assure him, then realize what I said. "Chicken breasts with vegetables," I clarify, closing and handing the waiter my menu.

God, this man is so fucking infuriating! I don't know why he gets under my skin so badly, but he does. It's like he knows exactly what's going on in my head, and I fucking hate it! I need some separation and air...

"Excuse me," I say to the table as I push my chair back and get to my feet, escaping to the bathroom while everyone else orders.

Thankfully, there's an empty stall, so I step inside and shut the door. Resting my back against one of the side walls, I close my eyes and blow out a frustrated breath to try and calm down.

What the hell is Pax talking about? How could he think I'm gay, just because I was alone in a locker room and watched porn with two men?

I like women. I'm physically attracted to women. When I said I wanted breasts, it was the truth! Tits and ass are the hottest things I've ever seen.

As I close my eyes, I try to think of a beautiful woman, one completely naked, laid on my bed. I would definitely fuck her, no doubt about it.

Right?

I'd love to stroke my dick between some big tits or...or fuck her doggy style. Yeah, and I could even be convinced to try having her warm wet mouth wrapped tight around my hard, aching length.

After my college debacle, I don't drink very often. So, the two drinks in my bloodstream are already making warmth spread all through me. That's the excuse I use for flattening my palm over the bulge in my jeans...

Vaguely, I hear the main bathroom door open, and someone comes in humming a song. Not just any song, but the *Jeopardy* tune as if they're searching for the answer to a question...

Paxton.

Even suspecting it's him just on the other side of the thin door, I'm not able to remove my hand from my dick. I'm a big guy soft, and now with it hard I need to take care of it or I won't be able to walk through the restaurant without getting strange looks or having people snap photos to post on social media.

Unzipping my jeans to ease the pressure, I can say that this is actually the first time I've had to relieve myself in public. For the past week, my dick has gone from limp to being desperate for more than my hand on it. The damn thing keeps popping up and needing a beating.

"Uh, Lathan? You do know the toilets are at the *back* of the stalls, right?" Pax's arrogant voice asks. And with all my blood rushing south, it takes me a moment to figure out what he's talking about.

Shit. He must be able to see my feet from underneath the stall and can tell they're sideways.

"Fuck off," I tell him since no other explanation is forthcoming with my hand on my dick.

"Are you...are you in there jerking off?" he asks, causing my face and neck to go up in flames.

"No!" I huff, trying to think of some excuse for my strained voice. "I think it's...it might be food poisoning."

Silence on the other side of the wall and then, "But we haven't eaten anything yet."

A growl of annoyance is my only response. And surprisingly my cock is not the least bit concerned with our conversation. In fact, it's getting harder, apparently liking having someone else in the room while being serviced.

"Can I watch?"

"Nooo!" I shout, and it comes out sounding pained when my cock jerks in my fist.

Oh. My. God. Did he seriously just fucking ask that? Who asks that sort of thing?

"You should hurry up before everyone starts wondering what you're up to in here," Pax adds helpfully. "Need a hand?"

"Oh, for fuck's sake," I groan when he quotes the goddamn porno.

That's about the time the unlatched stall door pushes inward, and Pax slips inside the small space with me.

"What the fuck are you doing?" I yell at him, fumbling to try and shove my hard dick into my boxer briefs and zip up. It's not easy to do over an enormous bulge.

"What? I thought you said, *'Oh, for fuck's sake'* like an agreement," Pax replies with a shrug, his dark eyes lowered to the crotch of my pants.

"Get out!" I tell him.

Ignoring me, he tsks and nods toward my denim teepee. "Well, you can't walk out of here like that."

"No shit," I mutter, scrubbing my hands over my embarrassed, red face.

"I don't usually do this, especially in Armani, *but*...take it out again, and I'll suck you off if you want," Pax says with a sigh. "I'll make it quick."

My hands fall from my face at the same time my jaw drops, looking at him to see if he seriously just offered to...

"I'm not –"

"Gay? So you've said," Pax interrupts and then pushes the sleeve of his jacket up to look at a sparkling watch on his wrist. "Besides, blowjobs are in the gray area. Man, woman, who cares how it gets done as long as you come, right?"

"What sort of fucked up logic is that?" I ask him, still unable to believe I'm in a public bathroom stall with another man.

"We can debate this later, but that's not getting any softer, is it?" he remarks while staring at my crotch.

"No," I agree, and it comes out nearly a groan because I'm hurting so badly in desperate need of relief. If my cock decides to be stubborn again, this could take an hour or more with my hand. My palm goes back down to the front of my jeans to apply pressure, and the next thing I know I'm unzipping and pulling it out.

"Wow," Pax murmurs. "Moby Dick looks awfully angry."

"Shut up and just do it already," I tell him as I start stroking my shaft again.

"You obviously don't have much experience getting a man on his knees," he grumbles. "Ask me nicely this time."

"Oh, my God," I groan up at the ceiling in frustration. But now that the idea of his mouth on me has been planted, there's no turning back. For once in my life, I need someone to touch me, dammit!

So, through gritted teeth, I ask, "Will you please suck me off?"

"Say my name," Pax adds.

"Asshole?" I offer up to the ceiling tiles. "Arrogant prick?"

When I see movement from the corner of my eye, I look down and realize he's opening the stall door. *Shit.*

Reaching past him to shut the door again with my palm, I cave. Shutting my eyes tightly, I force out the whispered words. "I need you, Pax, to suck my dick."

"Now, that wasn't so...*hard*, was it?" the annoying man asks with a grin before I look away in embarrassment.

Before I can grumble a smart-ass response, I feel the wet swipe of his tongue on my cockhead and nearly melt into a puddle on the floor. My eyes lower just in time to watch him fist the root of my dick in his grip and take me all the way into his mouth.

Nothing, and I mean *nothing*, has ever felt so amazing in my life. If I could bend over and kick myself in the ass for waiting this long to try another blowjob, I would. It's...mind-blowing. There's not even the slightest recoil from my stomach. Not a single thought of that night back in college. The warm, wet suctions are so good that my eyes roll back in my head, and a string of grunts and groans escape while this pain in the ass sucks my dick.

My only regret is that my first time is gonna be over way too soon.

CHAPTER 6

Pax

Paxton Price rarely gets on his knees, and he sure as fuck never does it in a two-thousand-dollar suit on a grubby public bathroom floor. But here I am, Lathan Savage's big whale of a dick plunging in and out of my mouth, once, twice, three times...

"Oh fuck! *Ohh,* fuck! *Ohhfffuuck*!"

That's the sound of a man coming if I've ever heard it before. And I have, plenty of times.

Since I don't want to make a mess on my suit, and for that reason only, I keep sucking as Lathan's cock jerks and pulses down my throat with his salty release. He's *so* going to owe me for this.

Straight, my tight ass. Bisexual maybe, but a truly straight man would've punched me in the face for walking in on him wanking off, not allowed me to stay, or caved when I made him ask for my mouth.

Speaking of tight ends, while Lathan's lost to the pleasure, I reach around with both hands and squeeze his clenching ass cheeks while he finishes in my mouth. Fuck, that's a mighty fine ass. The front of my pants grows tighter when all sorts of fantasies about fucking him fill my head. Holding his narrow hips while I thrust into him from behind...

"Stop, stop, stop, stop," Lathan utters urgently from above me when he grabs my hair and starts pulling me off of his dick.

"A little late for that," I remark as I make a show of wiping off my mouth with the back of my hand.

"Sorry," he says, and I prepare myself for the excuse that's forthcoming. "It's too...sensitive," is Lathan's surprising follow up, rather than the good old, *That was a mistake,* or *I was drunk.*

Getting to my feet, I make sure to stand close enough to him that he can feel my hard cock brush against his deflating one.

"I would ask for repayment now, but it'll take a lot more than three licks," I tell him. Since we're nearly the same height with Lathan slumping against the wall, our faces are only a breath apart.

Licking his lips, Lathan replies with, "It's just been awhile."

"Obviously," I reply.

"Fuck you," Lathan says with a shove to my chest to try and put room between us in the small space.

"You just did," I remark before I take that as my hint to leave.

Glancing at my watch as I walk out of the bathroom and adjust my hard shaft to make it less obvious in my suit pants, I realize that we've been gone for at least five minutes now. There's no way the others won't notice our joint absence.

As predicted, all of their eyes watch me retake my seat at the table. "Whew, long line," I lie to try and explain because, for whatever reason, I don't want Lathan to catch a bunch of shit from his friends.

With a nod, everyone seems to buy the excuse and goes back to their conversations. In fact, when Lathan returns to his seat, they thankfully don't even bat an eye at him.

His face is the color of a ripe tomato, but otherwise he seems fine, not freaking out nearly as much as one would expect from what I'm guessing was his first gay experience. If I have anything to say about it, though, it won't be his last.

So, after we finish eating and I sign my credit card receipt, I take the customer copy and write out a short message on the back of it. Then, discreetly, I fold and slide the paper across the table underneath Lathan's hand, making him startle and jerk it back. His eyebrows raise in question before his eyes cut to our friends to see if they noticed. Satisfied that they didn't, he picks up the piece of paper and reads it before slipping it into his pocket.

...

Lathan

"*Now you owe me one, tight end. P.S. Moby Dick was bigger and better than I imagined.*"

A few simple words with one helluva meaning behind them. Two sentences and my dick twitches remembering his hot mouth on it.

Below the comments is a phone number, followed by the name of his hotel, which is the same one the team is staying at, and a room number. Like I would ever consider showing up at some man's room for sex during an away game with all my teammates around. Not that I would if my teammates weren't around...

I'm grateful for the amazing blowjob, one I know I'll never regret since it was my first one to completion and without any vomit being involved. But that's it. This was a crazy, one-time thing that will never, ever happen again.

CHAPTER 7

Lathan

"You don't have to worry about cooking anything," I tell my mom on my cell phone as I drive home from practice.

"We have to cook something. It's our Thanksgiving tradition," my mom says weakly through the phone.

My throat grows scratchy with the realization that this very well may be her last Thanksgiving.

Clearing the emotion from my voice, I tell her, "Well, don't make a big fuss for me. And I can't wait to see you."

"We can't wait to see you either," she says softly. "Love you, Lathan."

"Love you too, Mom. Get some rest."

When I park in front of my townhouse, I blink back the tears and compose myself in case I run into any neighbors. It feels like all of my energy has been drained from me as I make the walk up the sidewalk. But one look at the welcome mat perks me up.

On first glance, it looks like a bouquet of flowers, and then I pick up the brightly colored bundle and realize it's...

"You've got to be fucking kidding me," I groan, glancing around nervously to see if any neighbors have seen them and are watching me right now.

No one is thankfully in sight, so I quickly unlock the townhouse door and slip inside with my gift.

If I thought the porn was shocking, it's nothing compared to the colorful arrangement of cock suckers. Actual cocks that are suckers.

They are five-inch cocks in various colors, placed on sticks. Suckers that are shaped like cocks, including miniature balls.

Finding the small envelope on the stand in the center, I carefully pull it off and open it, my heart racing, not knowing what I'll find inside.

The note says, "*I figured you might need some practice. Pay up soon, or I'll start sending these to the stadium. Don't worry; I'm local now to make it that much easier on you. And believe me, your efforts will be rewarded.*"

There's no signature, but there is an address. A Wilmington address.

My mind is blown for one that he expects me to...to do that for him, and also because he lives in fucking Wilmington now? When the hell did that happen?

He was supposed to be in Tennessee, safely hours away from me.

As my stomach growls, my musings come to an end, and I start thinking about what I can have for dinner.

The red, orange, yellow, green, blue and purple cock suckers look fruity and delicious, so I pull out the yellow one from the bouquet and peel off the wrapper.

Before I can talk myself out of it, I shove it into my mouth.

Mmm. Lemon flavored. Not bad. Yanking on the white stick, I pull it out, rubbing the sucker along my tongue to get a better taste.

That's when I realize there's no good way to lick a sucker without it being erotic. So, I say fuck it and go to town on one right after another. And surprisingly, all I can think about is what would Pax's dick taste like? And I'm sure Pax's cock would be a lot bigger than these lollipops.

So, by the time I get to the last two, the blue and purple, I double up, opening both of them and sucking on them at the same time. The fullness in my mouth makes my dick twitch, remembering how good it felt when Pax was on his knees, sucking me off.

His note said my efforts would be rewarded. Does that mean he would blow me again? God, it was so good that I think I could be talked into doing anything to feel his mouth on my cock one more time.

For the past four days, I've come home depressed about my mom's illness and exhausted from practice, but I'm never too tired to jerk off to the memory of Pax on his knees. The real thing is so much better.

CHAPTER 8

Pax

When the doorbell rings, I'm certain it's my Chinese takeout.

Imagine my surprise when I open the door and find Lathan fucking Savage on the other side, looking just as gorgeous as always with his closely trimmed, mussed blond hair wearing jeans and a tight blue tee that shows off his thick biceps and massive chest.

I can't believe he's here.

Ah, he must have gotten my cock suckers.

So, either he's going to punch me or...

"Come to pay up?" I ask, faking my bravado.

"Guess so," he says. "I'm here, aren't I?"

"Come in," I say.

Swallowing down my shock after hearing his easy agreement, I hold the door open only wide enough that Lathan's wide shoulder brushes my chest as he enters.

"Just move in?" he asks, although it's obvious based on the piles of cardboard boxes sitting around the living room instead of furniture.

"Yeah," I answer.

Before Lathan has time to think up more small talk or chicken out, I tell him, "Sit down."

"Ah, where?" he asks, glancing around the room.

"On a box."

"I doubt if they can hold me," he mutters.

"These are full of books; they can hold you," I assure him, pointing to the closest ones.

As soon as he lowers himself down slowly onto one, I undo my suit pants and pull my cock out of my boxer briefs.

"Whoa, wait a second," Lathan says, wide-eyed as he jumps to his feet again and puts up his hands in front of him. But he doesn't even try to look away from the dick in my hands.

"Wait for what? Isn't this what you came over here for?" I ask with a wave of my left hand to my growing length.

"Yeah, but, I've never done this before..."

"You'll learn as you go, and it's gonna take longer than three licks, so you better get started," I warn him. Gripping his shoulder, I shove him back down onto the box, and he goes without putting up any resistance.

The truth is, I'm already so hard just thinking about his virgin mouth that I may not last as long as Lathan did at that restaurant.

"The first step is to open your mouth," I tell him.

Swallowing so deeply I hear the actual *gulp*, Lathan quickly wets his bottom lip with his tongue. Then he opens his mouth wide...and I can't contain my bark of laughter.

"What?" he asks, his entire face suddenly turning crimson.

Dammit, that wasn't very nice of me.

"Sorry," I say, reaching for his shoulder again that's nice and hard and warm through his cotton shirt. "Your tongue is...is...bluish-purple –" Another round of laughter escapes before I can contain it.

"Fuck you," Lathan says, a favorite phrase of his when he's pissed I'm starting to recognize. With a rough shove to my stomach, he pushes me away to get to his feet and start for the door.

"Wait, dammit! I'm sorry, okay?" I yell to his retreating back while shoving my dick back into my boxer briefs. "I didn't think you would come, and I *really* didn't think you would eat the suckers."

"So, what? Is this all some game to you, making me look like a fool?" he turns around and asks, his stormy gray eyes swirling with fury. He's so big and angry and...so fucking hot. I would give anything to have him slam me against the wall and take out some of that aggression on me.

Wait, what?

No, that's not right. I can't believe that thought even crossed my filthy mind. *I* would be the one fucking all the hostility out of *him*.

"No, I'm not trying to make a fool of you," I assure him. That's likely impossible since even a colorful rainbow tongue looks good on this jock next door, golden boy. "I wanted you," I admit to try and explain why I've made an ass out of myself. "I *want* you," I clarify. "But I thought you would be like all the other jocks, too fucking stubborn to admit the truth to yourself and actually give me a chance."

"I'm not gay!" he declares through clenched teeth, those enormous hands made for grabbing balls, um, footballs out of the air, planted on his narrow hips.

"I know that. I get it. And it's okay to be attracted to women *and* men too, all right?" I tell him, figuring that his defensiveness at the moment is more about his questionable sexuality than my inappropriate laughter. "There are tons of bisexuals who like having sex with both genders, even if they prefer one over the other..."

"I wouldn't know. I've never done this before," Lathan mutters on a sigh with his eyes lowering, right along with his diffusing anger.

Now we're finally getting somewhere.

"So, the other night at the restaurant, that was your first time with a man?" I ask, needing confirmation. For whatever reason, I want to hear him say I'm the only guy to ever touch him.

"Yes," he answers, making me want to break out in a celebratory touchdown dance. "That's not...normal for straight men, is it?" he asks while eyeing my still unbuttoned pants again.

"No, not straight men," I admit. "Just men who like to sleep with men and women."

"But if I've never been with a woman, does that mean I'm gay?" he asks shyly, looking up at me through his golden lashes.

Wait a fucking minute. He doesn't mean...

"You're a virgin?" I ask, trying to keep the disbelief out of my voice.

Nodding, he says, "Yeah, I'm a fucking twenty-four-year-old virgin. Laugh all you want."

But I don't laugh because while it's shocking as shit that this gorgeous man has made it this long in his life without having a woman jump him, it's also very...endearing. Surely he's been faced with temptation more times than he can probably count, especially since he became a highly paid professional athlete. Yet every single time he had the strength and willpower to walk away.

"You must have fooled around with plenty of women, though, right?" I ask.

Another shake of his head.

Holy shit!

"So, the um, the other night, in the ah, bathroom," I stammer in complete disbelief. "That was the first time you...that you..."

"Came in someone's mouth?" Lathan supplies. "Yes. A girl tried before, but it was a disaster..."

Holy. Shit.

Those seem to be the only two words I can formulate after hearing this revelation.

And I would be lying if I said my chest wasn't puffed up like a proud peacock knowing I was the one who he caved for. Okay, so the night at the restaurant was likely just the result of twenty-four years of sheer horniness, but I would like to think I personally had something to do with it.

"Are you attracted to women?" I ask him.

"Hell yes," Lathan replies adamantly.

"Okay, well, the same applies," I assure him. "If you want to have sex with women and you want to fool around with men, then you're not gay. You're bisexual, if you're concerned about labels or whatever. If you were gay, women wouldn't even be a blip on your radar. At least that's how I feel."

"So you're..." he begins to ask.

"Gold-star gay, which means I've never been with a woman, and I'm certain that I never, ever will," I explain. "Well, unless there's a zombie apocalypse or a meteor hits Earth and mankind's dependent on me helping repopulate the world with the sole remaining female, then I guess I would do my duty, but I would seriously hate it..."

"Okay, I get it," Lathan says with an actual half-smile on his gorgeous face.

"If you want to do this with me, then don't talk yourself out of it," I tell him, coming back around to the reason this whole conversation started. "Because those urges won't go away, no matter what you do, or how many times you fuck a woman..."

"How would you know?" he asks with a furrowed brow.

"I know guys that try and repress their needs. It usually backfires. Badly."

"Oh," Lathan mutters. "Well, even if we...do this, I'm not agreeing to give up on women, or the pursuit of them."

"Not asking you to," I reply, even if the truth is I want every inch of his big, beautiful, untouched body all to myself.

"So, what do you want out of this?" he asks.

"You," I say honestly. "However I can get you, because you're sexy as fuck and I really want to get naked with you."

This time, when he glances away and blushes, I know he's not angry at me. He's shy and can't take a compliment.

"So, how about a compromise tonight?" I offer. "I'll suck your dick while you suck mine?"

"Same time?" he asks while grabbing at the collar of his shirt.

"Yeah, and that way, there's less pressure and attention on you. Just do to me whatever feels good for you."

"I, ah, okay," he stammers.

"Should we go to the bedroom?" I ask. "It will be more comfortable, and we'll have more room..."

"Yeah, all right," Lathan agrees but doesn't move.

"It's this way," I tell him, nodding over my shoulder down the hall. "I'm gonna go and start getting undressed. You can just join me when you're ready."

When I turn my back on the tight end and start for my bedroom, I figure there's a fifty-fifty chance that he'll follow me. Either that or he'll walk out the door and never look back.

In my bedroom, I flip on the lights so I don't trip over boxes and because I want to see all of him if he doesn't bolt. Then, I start unbuttoning my dress shirt. I'm on the last button when Lathan steps into the room.

"Should I...undress?" he asks nervously from behind me.

"If you want to, that's up to you, but I would like to see you naked," I encourage.

It's not a moment later when I hear the sound of clothes rustling, telling me he's thankfully taking something off. Even if it's just his shoes, I'll be thrilled to make progress.

I still can't believe he's a fucking virgin, not with just men but with women too.

That's when an idiotic thought hits me.

Maybe, just maybe, if I can show him how amazing things could be between us, he won't ever end up being one of those guys who have relationships with women and just fucks me on the side. It's a long shot, I know, but one I still want to pursue.

Unable to wait any longer, I turn around to get a look at him and...

"Holy...fucking...wow," I mutter at the sight. Tall, muscular, and perfectly tan all over with a long, thick dick that appears very happy to see me, I don't think I've ever seen anyone as incredible looking as the man before me. "How are you...how are you still a virgin?" I ask. Lathan's a professional athlete, making a ton of money, and he's gorgeous. It doesn't make sense.

"Just haven't found the right woman," he says with a shrug, his face and neck turning red again.

"Right woman?" I repeat because that's a first. Most young, single, straight or bi men don't care how "right" they are as long as their legs spread.

"I never know what to say or do," he admits.

Jesus, he's shy. Hasn't he ever seen himself in a mirror?

"Just a wild guess," I tell him. "But you probably wouldn't have to say or do anything to get laid."

"It's just, everyone is so experienced, and I'm...not," he replies, crossing his arms over his chest, protectively, like he's trying to hide his body from my view.

"I can help you with experience," I assure him. "You know, if you want to get some practice?"

"You would do that?" he asks. "Without laughing at me again?"

"I only laughed before because your mouth was bluish-purple and it caught me by surprise," I remind him.

That's the point at which I realize I won't be getting a blowjob tonight. If Lathan had been an ass and not opened up to me, then yeah, maybe I would've put him on his knees and told him to suck me off, but he did admit that he's inexperienced. And based on his shyness, I'm guessing I shouldn't rush him into anything. We need to take things slow. Ease him into physical intimacy so that he doesn't get scared and bolt.

"Why don't we just take things slowly?" I suggest. "If I had known...well, I wouldn't have sucked your dick in a public restroom like that. Honestly, I'm surprised you didn't run out the door and say to hell with dinner afterward."

"I may have been uptight before...but after...after I was embarrassed and worried someone would find out, sure, but I didn't regret it," he tells me, his gray eyes so sincere and honest that I could kiss him.

So I do.

Closing the small distance between us, I reach up and grab the back of Lathan's neck since he's a few inches taller and pull his mouth down to mine. His full lips are nice and damp, the kiss hesitant and soft at first until he relaxes and grabs my neck the same way, pulling me to him even closer. As soon as our hard cocks brush against each other, both of us groan.

Using the opportunity to deepen the kiss, I slip my tongue against Lathan's, and all hell breaks loose. His shy, timidness from before disappears, and the next thing I know, the vigor of his frantic tongue retaliation is forcing me backward. Down onto the bed we fall with Lathan's heavy body on top of mine. It's obvious that he likes the change in position based on how hard his dick is pressing into my stomach.

Reaching between us, I wrap my hand around both of our shafts and start stroking them together, his hot, velvety, rock hard dick rubbing against my own. I don't know if it's my pre-cum or his that wets my hand, but I use the slickness to jerk us faster.

Our kiss grows more desperate each second until we're panting into each other's mouths. Tongues are bitten, teeth clash, and it's so fucking good. No one has ever kissed me with this type of intensity. Sure, there have been plenty of passionate ones when we fuck, but not like how Lathan attacks me like a wild, ravenous beast.

His palms continue gripping my face between them as his hips buck, fucking my fist harder. I'm getting close myself. My balls are drawn up tight to my body, and my ass is already clenching.

A knock at the door nearly pulls me back from my release, but it doesn't seem to faze Lathan. With a curse, he buries his face in my neck as his warm, sticky release spills over my hand and onto my dick. His masculine growls and grunts are so sexy before he sinks his teeth into my shoulder, sending me over the edge.

I yell out, "I'm coming! I'm fucking coming!" as the pleasure rushes down my spine, through my balls and erupts from my dick. And while I'm vaguely aware of the Chinese guy at my front door, what's most surprising is that in the heat of the moment we just shared, if Lathan had asked, I would've let him fuck me without the least bit of hesitation. Damn if that's not a disturbing thought.

"*Fuuuck*," I groan while my fist milks my cock to the last drop. "Fuck."

Releasing our two soggy shafts, I throw my arms above my head in surrender and try to remember how to breathe even with a big ass tight end still on top of me.

At the sound of another knock, I pat Lathan's shoulder and tell him, "Sorry, but I need to get up."

"Yeah...okay," he replies between pants before he rolls off of me and onto the bed.

When I get up to clean myself up and throw on my clothes, or at least enough to be presentable, I can't stop myself from glancing over at Lathan's naked, sweaty body, sprawled out across most of my king-sized bed. His semi-hard cock lying on his beautiful washboard abs is just begging to be sucked back into commission.

"What?" Lathan asks, sounding grumpy before he sits up on the side of the bed and reaches for his boxer briefs.

"I was just thinking that I could spend days running my mouth all over you," I tell him honestly while pulling a tee over my head. "Be right back. That's my Chinese food."

CHAPTER 9

Lathan

After Pax walks out of his bedroom to answer the front door, my elbows dig into my knees so I can rest my head in my hands, trying to get my wits about me again.

I don't even know what the fuck just happened.

Only my best friend, Quinton, knows the extent of my experience, and yet I just spilled every single embarrassing detail to Pax, a man I barely know. One who can apparently put his hands or mouth on me and make me come like a teenager.

I'm not sure what came over me, but there was something exciting about the way we kissed that I just lost control of myself. All I know was that I wanted to be on top of him and couldn't wait any longer. There was this...urge to bury myself inside him that I've never felt before. Watching porn, I've jerked myself off plenty of times, but never did I imagine needing to be in those women. Or men. Honestly, I don't even think I really noticed the men in the movies, so why do I get so turned on with Pax?

Of course, he's attractive; that's not even debatable. He's tall and lean with a pretty face, neatly trimmed facial hair, nice kissable lips and comforting chocolate eyes unless he's laughing or smirking at me...

And yeah, I'm not really in the mood to hear him even joke around about how fast I came, so I slip my shoes on and start thinking of excuses to leave as I make my way into the kitchen. That's where I find Pax, his back to me and a brown bag of food on the counter.

"So, um, I've got to get going," I tell him.

"Okay," he says without even a hint of surprise or disappointment.

"Guess I'll see you later," I say.

"Yeah, sure," he replies, still not bothering to face me before I let myself out.

On the way to my Jeep, I can't help but wonder if I did something wrong or if maybe Pax is just that casual about screwing around.

Although, I guess I do still owe him a blowjob, but I'm glad he didn't insist I do it tonight. I would've; it's just, I have no clue how to do it. Since I've only had one and a half in my entire life, that's not much to go on. Guess it's time to try and watch that part of pornos again.

So, that's what I do when I get home.

Or maybe I just want to see some pussy to assure myself that I'm not gay after having a man's hands on me.

Pulling out my go-to DVD, *The Naughty Girl Next Door,* I pop it into my computer and start it up. If I can jerk myself off watching this, I'll feel better about everything going on in my head, and then I can finally get a shower to clean up the stickiness. Stickiness left behind from when my dick was being stroked against Pax's cock. Pushing those memories aside, I stretch out on my back on the bed next to the laptop and click the play button.

Like most porn, things heat up fast. The dude starts playing with the college girl's fake tits through her shirt, and then he takes them out and sucks on her nipples. While that's great and all, I'm ready to get to the part I'm most worried about, so I hit the fast-forward arrow and let it skip ahead to the end.

After the naughty girl gets fucked for a while, she gets off the bed and goes to her knees at the footboard. The guy steps forward with his cock long and stiff to shove it into her mouth, making her moan before she grips the base and starts bobbing her head while jerking him off.

It takes some work, but I get my cock hard again. I can't come before the guy on the screen finishes, spurting all over the girl's expectant face. I don't get why in porn the man always does that when I know for a fact that it felt so damn good to come in Pax's throat while he kept up the suction.

Oh yeah. That gets my dick twitching in interest. So, I close my eyes and think about that night in the restaurant in Tennessee. Pax on his knees in his immaculate suit, his hand and mouth working me over, so hot and confident. The best part was, based on his enthusiasm and effort, I think he *liked* doing it. God, it was so good to have his wet mouth on me. That's why I couldn't last long. I came so fucking hard...

My dick jerks in my hand, and then my hips are pumping right through my orgasm that's short and sweet since I just came earlier tonight.

Fuck.

Now I know why it's been so hard for me to find a release lately. It's not just the stress and anxiety apparently. Heterosexual porn just doesn't do it for me like gay porn or thinking about being with Pax. I guess it's time to finally face the fact that, while I may not normally get aroused by men, he does it for me. There's no denying that fact, as much as I hate to admit it to myself.

Pax was right. I'm bisexual, and right now I want him. That's nothing to be ashamed of. No one has to know what the two of us do behind closed doors. As long as I go to his place at night, none of his neighbors will likely recognize me. Besides, paparazzi don't follow me around or anything. I'm a boring virgin that's never seen in public with a woman on my arm. I don't get drunk or crazy either, so there's nothing for them to report in their sleazy papers.

I like the way I feel when I'm with Pax, and hopefully, he wants to keep seeing me. Tonight, we didn't part on great terms, but that's probably my fault for up and leaving so quickly.

If I want to be with him, though, I need to be prepared to give, not just receive. Otherwise, he'll get fed up and move on to someone else who will take care of all his needs. That's definitely not what I want to happen. Even though it may be a little scary, and way out of my comfort zone, I'll keep practicing and figure out what the hell to do, starting with a blowjob. Pax offered to let me experiment with him, and he didn't laugh at me when I told him I was a virgin.

So, after I take a quick shower and get ready for bed, I grab my cell phone and the receipt I kept with his phone number on it to type out a text message.

Tomorrow night I want you to teach me how to suck your dick.

Before I can talk myself into deleting it, I hit send. Then, I hold my breath and wait for a response.

Fuck. What if I sent the message to the wrong number? Or if I was wrong about him wanting to see me again?

The three dots suddenly appear on the screen, telling me that Pax is typing a response. It's one word.

Great.

I don't have time to wonder if he means that or if he's being sarcastic when the next message comes in.

Now I'll have to jerk off before I can go to sleep.

That's a good thing, right? He's admitting that he's turned on by my words?

Encouraged by that I decide to respond.

Me too. Just finished.

The three dots appear again, but I think I can guess what his reply will be, so I go ahead and answer it.

Your mouth in the bathroom. Don't think I'll ever forget it and I don't want to. Now I need to repay the favor.

The dots disappear for several long moments before they reappear again.

Tomorrow night. Can't wait.

The two short sentences are followed by a winking emoticon that makes me smile.

Still grinning like an idiot, I tell him, **See you then**, before I put my phone away and try to get some sleep.

CHAPTER 10

Pax

"Hey, you've got furniture," Lathan says when he walks into my house for the second night in a row.

"Yeah, it was just delivered," I say coolly like I haven't jerked off twice today thinking about him saying he wanted to come over and suck my cock. Sure, he said that last night but that was under duress, my threat of sending cock suckers to the stadium. Not that I would do that, but I wanted to light a fire under the tight end's ass. And it worked. He showed up, and then I found out he was more inexperienced than I thought.

Tonight, though, he's here because he wants to be. And if he offers it again, I won't be able to turn him down.

"Have a seat," I tell him. "You want anything to eat or drink?" I ask to try and give him time to get comfortable.

"Nah, I'm good," he says, still standing in the entryway, so I lead him over to the living room and take a seat on my new, beige leather sofa.

"Okay, well, come try out my new furniture," I suggest rather than give in to my dick that wants to insist that we go straight to the bedroom and get started.

"It looks nice," Lathan says while standing in front of me on the sofa. Reaching down, he lifts his Wildcats hoodie over his head and off, causing his tee to ride up and tease me with a view of his sexy abs.

"Don't stop there," I say, unable to help myself.

"Huh?" he mutters with a creased forehead before asking, "Oh. Should I take my shirt off too?"

"Yes," I encourage. "You work hard for that body; someone should be able to appreciate it."

Now blushing, Lathan obliges, grabbing the hem and removing the cotton shirt in one swift move. That broad chest, thick biceps, and six pack abs deserve to be in a museum somewhere, the Fine As Fuck Hall of Fame.

"That's much better," I tell him while stroking the growing bulge in my pants so that he knows I *really* like what I see. The front of Lathan's jeans also seem a little snug all of a sudden. "Keep going. Get comfortable," I suggest as I unbutton and unzip my pants to allow for further expansion. Much needed expansion I realize when Lathan follows through and takes off his shoes, pants, and socks.

"Gorgeous," I tell him when he stands before me in nothing but black boxer briefs that are stretched tight over his Moby Dick. That's when I finally notice that my hand has disappeared into my underwear, trying to take care of my own stiffy.

"Pull it out," Lathan orders, his deep voice huskier than usual and his eyelids growing heavier when I comply.

"He really wants you to come give him a kiss," I tell him, jerking myself slowly with a firm stroke down and back up the shaft.

Without further encouragement, Lathan steps forward and goes down to his knees between my spread thighs, landing so hard the whole house rattles. When his tongue darts out and wets his lips, I ask, "You want it?"

"Yes," he replies hoarsely.

"Then take it. Kiss my cock like you kissed me last night," I tell him, removing my hand and letting my length slap against my stomach.

Tentatively, Lathan lifts his hands and rubs them up the top of my thighs before easing them underneath my shirt. He keeps pushing the material up my chest and off.

"Holy fuck!" I exclaim, my hips punching forward and my entire body shuddering when, without warning, I feel Lathan's hot tongue licking up the underside of my cock right before my shirt even clears my head. I never even saw it coming.

His big hands squeeze my hips and then jerk my lower body toward him, leaving me slumping on the sofa when the real torture begins.

Keeping his hands on my sides, Lathan uses only his mouth on my dick, licking me from root to tip, swirling his tongue around my dripping head. His touches are feather light, the perfect tease. Then, he pulls one of his hands from me to jerk down the elastic waistband of my boxer briefs even further to bury his face in my crotch.

"*Uh, fuck yesss*!" I yell, throwing my head back and lifting my hips when the tip of his tongue flicks rapidly against my sensitive sac, over and over again. My balls shoot upward toward my body to prepare for release, and he hasn't even sucked my cock yet. Gritting my teeth, I grab two fistfuls of the top of my jeans to try and hold it off a little longer. But when he latches his mouth over my left nut and sucks, I'm a goner.

"Fuck! Gotta come," I warn Lathan, who lifts his head to look up at me in confusion right before my dick erupts. "Jerk me off. Please jerk me off," I beg him as my body seizes.

He takes me in his hand and starts stroking through my release while my eyes roll back in my head and I groan in pleasure.

"I did it wrong," Lathan says right when I start to float back down, so it takes a few seconds to figure out what the hell he's talking about.

"No, you didn't," I assure him, reaching for his jaw just to touch him in some little way to try and show my gratitude. "That was...definitely right."

"But I didn't even get to taste you," he says before he grips my base in his fist and leans forward to lick the cum from my dick, sending tingles shooting up my spine. I figure one taste would be plenty for him to get his fill, but nope. Lathan laps at me until I'm so clean I'm hard again. That's when he looks up at me, opens wide, and starts sucking me off.

I come again for the second time in less than five minutes of his head bobbing and fist pumping.

"Wow," I mutter as I melt deeper into the leather cushions, content and high on endorphins. Grabbing his chin, I tell him, "This mouth is a gift from God, sent down to Earth for the sole purpose of pleasuring men."

"I'm not gay," he replies, not quite as tersely as last night.

"Doesn't mean it's not true," I tell him when I let his face go. "I've had guys suck my dick for half an hour without being able to make me come."

"Half an hour?" Lathan asks from where he's still kneeling in front of me. "You can last that long."

"Not with you apparently," I remark, remembering how fast I blew my load yesterday too. "You're really good at sucking dick to be a virgin."

"I just did what I would want to be done to me," he replies, reaching down to adjust himself. Poor man. After that performance, he deserves to get his own O-face.

"Take your underwear off and get up here," I tell him, smacking the top of my thighs to show him where I want him.

"What?" he asks, but he gets to his feet and shoves his boxer briefs down as commanded. His long length is jutting out thick and proud.

"Climb up," I tell him, patting my thighs again.

On a long sigh, Lathan reaches for the top of the sofa to steady himself as he straddles my lap. Just as I expected from how I'm slumping, his cock is poised right at face level, so I wrap my hand around his shaft and bring him forward into my mouth.

"Oh God," Lathan moans before his hips start bucking, wanting to fuck my mouth. I keep my grip on the halfway point of his big dick to keep him from choking me, but let him have at it. He pumps hard and fast like he's desperate for a release while his salty flavor leaks onto my tongue.

"*Oh fuck! Oh! Oh God! I'm gonna...*" His groans turn into wordless grunts as he slams one last time into my mouth and his hot release pulses down my throat. I reach down and cup his balls while he finishes and then grab a handful of his bare ass just because I can. It's so nice and tight I want to slap it while I'm balls deep fucking him.

That's probably getting way ahead of myself here, but I can't help it. A virgin ass this nice needs to be claimed. And if anyone is going to take it, it's going to be me.

...

Lathan

My second blowjob was even better than my first. Probably because I wasn't so uptight about it. Here, in the privacy of Pax's place, I could let go, relax, and enjoy every second instead of worrying about who will find out.

Another reason it was better could be because I was twice as hard and ready to blow than that first night. I had no idea that going down on Pax would turn me on so much, but it did. I liked having my mouth on his hard cock, making him scream and writhe while losing control. Hell, I didn't even mind his salty, chlorine flavor like the ocean and pool all mixed together.

And now I'm still slumped on Pax's lap and know I should move to let him breathe, but I can't make myself climb off of him just yet. The warmth of our skin-to-skin contact is nice and comforting, and not something I've ever experienced with anyone before. Although, Pax is likely suffocating since his face is now pressed into my stomach since I'm sitting back on my knees.

"My bed has more room," Pax eventually mutters.

"Okay," I agree since I'm not ready to leave and go home just yet. "But I can't stay much longer," I warn him.

"Yeah, I know," he agrees.

I finally force myself to climb off of him, stopping at the bathroom in the hallway to clean up, but I don't redress before I get in bed with Pax, who's already under the covers. He looks exhausted, his eyes barely squinting open at me when I roll over toward him.

"There's nothing gay about cuddling," he mumbles before throwing an arm over my waist and pressing his now naked body against the length of mine. Following his lead, I drape my arm over his side and tell myself that I'm only going to close my eyes and rest for a few minutes.

...

"Morning," Pax whispers when he wakes me up. Or, rather, his mouth kissing my chest and sending waves of pleasure to my cock wakes me up.

Wait, did he say *morning*?

I shoot up in the middle of the bed and start blinking my eyes open, glancing around for a clock and finding none. But the room is sunlit, so it's probably after seven.

"What time is it?" I ask, scrambling out of bed and wandering in a circle, looking for my phone before I remember it's in my pants in the living room. On the way there, I pass a wall clock that says it's nine-fucking-fifteen. Nine-fifteen!

"Fuck, fuck, fuck!" I shout as I quickly throw my clothes back on.

"Running late?" Pax asks from across the room. I barely spare a glance at him between the time it takes to pull my jeans up, but it's impossible to miss the fact that his hair is adorably mused, he's naked, and he's very hard.

"Yes, I'm late! Coach is gonna chew my ass up for it too," I say on the way to the door. "See you later?" I pause only long enough to ask because despite how late I am, I don't want to leave on bad terms after how nice staying here was. Sleeping with someone all night for the very first time was incredible, even better than the blowjob. The warmth and comfort were unlike anything I've ever imagined, and I want to do it again.

"Just call or text me," Pax wanders over and says. With both hands, he pulls my face to his for a quick kiss on the lips before he releases me and slaps my ass.

"Now get," he tells me with a sleepy grin, and I do, even though my feet are reluctant to move.

CHAPTER 11

Pax

"So, what do you think of this place?" Ana, the young, raven-haired realtor, asks with a wave of her hand. "It's not oceanfront like you wanted, but it's second row and has the pool surrounded by a sunroom so it can be used year-round."

"I love it," I tell her, walking over to look out the upstairs window to see the ocean. Honestly, she could've shown me a shack today and I probably would've liked it. That's just the effect a certain tight end staying the night has on me.

"Would you like to make an offer, or do you need some time to think about it?" she asks.

"I don't need any time. Let's put the offer in today," I reply, because this place is better than I even imagined. It's huge with open ceilings to make it look even more spacious, just what I need to fill it up with people without it feeling too crowded.

Smiling broadly, Ana says, "Great, I'll meet you back at the office."

Now that I've found the location, and assuming the seller accepts my offer, I can finally start planning. A few renovations will need to be made to open up the second floor. There are business and liquor licenses I'll need to apply for. We'll need furniture, a small staff, security. The list seems to go on and on and the work will be endless, but I'm excited. Soon, I'll have something that's all mine.

I wouldn't mind making Lathan all mine either.

My phone buzzes in my pocket; and when I pull it out, I'm surprised to see it's a text from Lathan who is supposed to be at practice until this afternoon.

Can I come over tonight? I'll bring dinner.

Three nights in a row, huh? I'm shocked. But he's bound to be horny after keeping it in his pants for this long. I will gladly get the tight end off as many times as he wants, especially after I found out just how talented his virgin mouth is.

I send back, **I'll text you when I get home, and dinner is your choice since I'm betting you worked up an appetite today.**

...

Lathan

I stay distracted at practice, playing like shit during every drill. And after Coach made me run five miles when everyone else was finished for the day to punish me for being late, I'm exhausted.

After getting Pax's response to my text message during our lunch break, I spent hours wanting to reply and ask where he was and what he was doing, waiting for him to say he's home. That's stupid, right?

Why do I even care what he does during the day? The two of us... well, that's physical and nothing else.

Pax said he's been out since high school. So, based on his looks and outgoing personality, I'm betting that he's had quite a few lovers. Hell, more than a few. So while I love being with him, at the same time I worry that I look like an inexperienced fool. Not just that, but I'm an overeager inexperienced fool who won't be enough for him.

That's why I've decided I'm not going to screw around with Pax tonight. It seemed like a great plan, showing him that I can be around him for more than five minutes without my dick getting hard. But then he opens his door, and I'm awestruck at the sight of him.

Like usual, he's wearing a suit, or what's left of it. The jacket is off, leaving him in his blue button down and dark pants, both of which mold to his lean body. Not a single one of his auburn hairs swept over to the left are out of place. He's so hot he's already making me throw wood. I use the bags of Chinese food in front of me to hopefully shield my reaction to him.

"Hey," he says. "You okay? You look a little spaced out."

"Hey, yeah, I'm fine," I answer.

"What's in the bags?" he asks.

"General Tso's chicken, dumplings, and egg rolls," I reply. The other night I remembered Pax ordered Chinese takeout, so I assumed it was a safe choice to pick up. "Any of that work?"

"That's great, thanks," he replies, stepping back so I can enter the house. "Do you wanna eat before or after?"

"Before or after what?" I ask on the way to the kitchen.

"Guess that depends on what you need tonight. But if I were a betting man, I would put my money on a blowjob."

Zing!

My cock jerks and lengthens to the point of pain behind my zipper. Still, I tell Pax, "That's not why I came over," even if it is a partial truth.

"Really?" he asks, sounding skeptical as he follows me to the kitchen. "Then you just came for dinner?"

"Yeah," I reply, glancing around the room to avoid his gaze and losing count of cardboard boxes. "That and to help you unpack. How do you move around in here?" I ask him.

"You're gonna help me unpack?" he says slowly.

"Why not?"

"We're gonna eat, you're gonna help me unpack after running yourself ragged at practice, and you don't even want me to suck your dick to show my gratitude?"

My restraint not only snaps in half, that motherfucker disintegrates.

"Well, when you put it that way," I reply with a grin when I finally meet his dark stare. "I won't require any sexual favors, but I wouldn't decline any that you deem appropriate."

"It's the least I can do," he says. "You still have years of oral to catch up on before you've hit the average for the rest of the world's population."

Climbing up on a stool to eat at the bar, I wince in pain and have to reach down to readjust myself. "You're like Viagra," I admit to him. "Keeping myself in check has never been a problem until I started hanging around you."

"It's the Pavlov effect," Pax replies as he spins my chair around to face him and his hands start undoing my pants. "Your cock knows who takes care of it, so it's always begging me to give it more attention."

"I think you're right," I agree, unable to contain my groan when he pulls my dick free and bends over to take it into his mouth. "You don't...you don't have to..." I try to say between gasps.

Pulling off my dick, he says, "I don't have to what? Make you feel good? Keep Moby Dick wet?" He strokes my cock while he talks, so I can barely keep up. "I know I don't have to, but I want to. So shut up and fuck my mouth so we can eat and you can help me unpack without being in pain."

I get to my feet and grab a handful of Pax's perfect hair, loving how I get to make it messy while watching my cock slide into his mouth that's stretched open as far as it will go.

...

Pax

Lathan lasts a little longer every time I blow him, which I sort of hate. It's fun to see how fast I can make him come. Tonight, I'm on my knees, letting him take control, pumping his hips as fast as he wants down my throat. His gray eyes don't close but watch me with heavy lids. When he tugs my head forward, I go as far as I can until I gag. He's got a big cock, so I doubt I'll ever be able to take every inch. Such a shame really.

"Pax...fuck," he moans as his eyes shut and he throws his head back. His fingers tighten in my hair and then he's coming, so I relax my throat, breathe through my nose and take every drop. It's not as big of a load as last night and definitely less than the first one.

When I take all that he gives me, I pull off and wipe my mouth. "Did you jerk off today?" I ask curiously.

"What? Why?" he asks when he jerks away to zip up.

"You did, didn't you? There's nothing wrong with that, Lathan. I did too, I was just wondering if you were thinking about me when you..."

"Yes," he answers. "In the shower, when I got home from practice."

"Good," I tell him with a smug smile as I get to my feet. "Now let's eat. I'm starving."

CHAPTER 12

Pax

Lathan and I are sitting on the sofa in my now organized house, watching a movie like a normal couple, and it's... nice. For a week now, he's been coming over every afternoon, bringing dinner with him since neither of us cooks, and of course fooling around with me. My only complaint is that every night we fall asleep together, all happy and cuddled up with legs entwined and our warm bodies pressed against each other, and then I wake up in the early morning cold and alone.

That's why tonight when Lathan's hand rubs up my thigh and he starts kissing my neck, I snap.

"Why do you keep sneaking out?" I ask him, sliding over to the next sofa cushion to put space between us.

"Huh?" he asks with his forehead creased adorably in confusion.

"Every night after we...enjoy each other, everything is great and we fall asleep, but then you disappear!"

"That's because I can't stay," he answers. "You know that. I have to get up early, and the last time I slept here I was ten minutes late to practice."

"Then why not just leave right after instead of getting my hopes up?" I ask, aware that I sound like a woman, which is concerning, yet my feelings still matter, so I go with it.

"Because I can't," he answers, scooting to the edge of the sofa and hanging his head.

"Yeah, you can!" I argue. "You get up, put your clothes on, and say thanks for the orgasm, I'm out."

"No, I meant that I don't want to leave right away. I just want to..."

"Want to what?" I snap.

"I just want to hold you for a little while, okay?" he says when he gets to his feet, clearly trying to escape from the admission he just dropped on me. And yeah, I felt a flutter in my stomach at hearing him say he stays for something more than sex.

"I want you to stay," I tell him. "Why can't you just set the alarm on your phone?" I ask. "Hell, I could set mine too just to make sure you wake up in time."

"You don't think anyone will see me leaving?" he asks softly, getting to his real concern.

"It's the offseason for the coast, so most of my neighbors' houses are vacant. I think you would be okay, especially if you wear a hat or pull up your hoodie."

"Okay," he agrees, still not facing me. "But I have to leave by eight."

"Eight. Got it. I'll set my phone now," I tell him, glad that it was so easy to convince him to stay.

I start to reach for my phone when my stomach suddenly lurches again, and I begin to think it doesn't have anything to do with the conversation. Nope, I'm pretty sure the flounder I had for dinner is trying to jump ship.

"Oh, God," I groan before racing to the bathroom. I barely make it to the toilet in time.

...

Lathan

It takes me a few minutes after Pax runs off before I realize what's happening.

Fuck.

He's sick.

And now I may barf thinking about him barfing.

I swallow down the instant nausea of my weak stomach and ease toward the bathroom in the master bedroom.

"Pax?" I call out. "You okay?"

His response is to call Ralph. And, boy, does he call old Ralph over and over again. The sound is enough to make me gag, so I go out to my Jeep and find my headphones. Once they're plugged into my phone, I turn on some Fall Out Boy, blast the volume and go back into the house.

Pax's head is still hanging in the toilet, so I open up the bathroom closet and grab a washcloth to wet it with cold water for him and then place it on the back of his neck. Turning my back to him, I remove my right earplug and ask, "Can I get you anything?"

"Nooo," he groans before more vomiting ensues.

Not sure what else to do, I step back into the bedroom and sit on the edge of the bed to listen to more songs.

When I get through the majority of an album, I get up to check on Pax again. He's still on the floor, his back slumped against the wall with the washcloth I gave him draped over his face.

"Pax?" I say. "Are you feeling any better?"

"Uh-uh," he replies.

Noticing a speck of vomit on his shirt, I say, "Can I help you get changed?"

"Uh-huh," he answers.

So, I squat down and start unbuttoning his shirt, careful to avoid the puke stain. Just as I start to pull his sleeve off, Pax lurches forward and starts getting sick again. I'm too close to ground zero this time with nothing to drown out the sound.

Quickly jumping up and sprinting to the bathroom in the hall, I lose all the shrimp and baked potato I had for dinner. The good news is that's the only time I get sick.

...

Pax

I wake up in bed, sweating, shivering and feeling like a big pile of dog shit. When I roll to my side, I see Lathan sound asleep facing me.

He stayed. Even when I was so fucking sick, he stayed.

That's when I notice that I'm wearing a Wildcats sweatshirt Roxy gave me and some jogging pants over my boxers. Since I would never, ever pick out this particular outfit to wear even in my own home, I know Lathan must have dressed me. I'm grateful for the warmth since I'm still trembling from what must be a fever. Fuck, I don't remember ever feeling this bad before.

My mouth is so dry and gross that it's worth risking more sickness to try and keep down some water, so I roll over and push my weak arms into a sitting position.

"What do you need?" Lathan asks, his voice groggy.

"Just gonna get some water," I tell him. "Go back to sleep." If I remember correctly, I'm pretty sure he was sick throwing up a few hours ago too.

"I've got it," he says before he's up and gone, disappearing out of the room. He comes back a minute later and hands me a bottle of water, wearing just his boxers. Even as ill as I am I can still appreciate his body.

"Thanks," I tell him before I take a sip. "How are you feeling?"

"I'm fine," he replies as he walks around to get back on his side of the bed.

"Weren't you sick too?" I ask, wondering if I imagined it.

"It was nothing," he grumbles.

"We must have a virus because we didn't even eat the same thing," I remark.

"Are you feeling better?" he asks.

"Yeah, surprisingly," I admit, as the water goes down without landing like a brick in my stomach.

"Then it's probably food poisoning," Lathan replies with his eyes closed.

"But I had flounder and you had shrimp..."

"My food was fine. I just get sick whenever I'm around people getting sick," he admits.

"Oh," I mutter. "Then why didn't you just leave?"

"Because I was worried about you," he says, opening his stormy eyes. "I didn't want to leave you alone."

"That is so...fucking sweet," I tell him, lying back down and reaching for his arm to give it a squeeze. "Thank you."

"Welcome. Now go back to sleep. You must be exhausted," he declares.

"Yeah, I am," I reply. "Night."

"Night," he says. "Wake me up if you need me."

If that was the case, then Lathan wouldn't ever get to sleep, because I'm starting to want and need him all the time.

CHAPTER 13

Lathan

"Feeling better?" I ask Pax when I walk into his place.

"Yeah, I am. Thanks. I think you were right. It was so quick I think it had to have been food poisoning."

"No more Captain Joe's then, huh?" I reply.

"Fuck Captain Joe," Pax agrees. Grabbing my biceps, he says, "Come here. I swear I've brushed my teeth like twenty times since last night."

I slant my lips over his for a few sweet kisses before our tongues begin to tangle.

"Bedroom?" he asks.

"Fuck yes," I agree. "If you're sure you feel like it..."

Pax grabs my hand and covers the bulge at the front of his pants with it. "What does that feel like?"

"Lead the way," I tell him.

In the bedroom, we undress each other. And then I push Pax

down on the bed to climb on top of him, which I love. As we make out, we end up on our sides, which is also great because it means I have easy access to grab his tight ass while our cocks rub against each other. When neither of us can take anymore, Pax grips our two shafts in his hand and gives us both a release.

While his hand is great, and his mouth is euphoric, I still find myself fantasizing about...more.

"I wanna fuck you," I blurt out, causing Pax's lips to freeze over my nipple before he lifts his head to look at me.

"No."

"No?" I repeat.

"No." Again, that one word answer from him is sharp and crisp, leaving no room for discussion.

"I don't understand," I say with my forehead creased in confusion. "Isn't that what gay men do?" I ask him.

"Not all of us," Pax replies before he rolls away and throws his legs over his side of the bed. "Some guys bottom and some top. Plenty even do both," he explains before looking at me over his shoulder. "I don't bottom. Ever."

"Oh, so you..." I start to say when the realization hits me. "No fucking way!" I exclaim. "You're not gonna fuck me. Is that what you expect?" I ask as I scramble out of bed to get dressed. There's no way he's...nope. No. Fucking. Way.

"You could at least think about it," Pax replies, standing up to pull his blue boxer briefs back on. "All of this is new to you, so how do you know you wouldn't like it?"

"How do you know *you* wouldn't like it?" I throw his question back at him while pulling on my jeans.

"Because I've done some ass play and didn't really see its appeal," he answers with a shrug as his head disappears into a white tee, ruffling his auburn hair and making him look even hotter than usual.

"Well, why would *you* think I would like it?" I ask with my hands on my hips, not bothering with a shirt because I like the way Pax eye fucks my chest and abs every time he looks in my direction. Now I know how women feel about men staring at their breasts, but I don't mind the attention. It's nice to feel attractive and wanted after spending most of my life having a revolting body.

"You don't know if you like something until you try it," he replies. "Besides, I know your type."

"*My* type?" I repeat. "I'm a type?"

"Yeah," Pax says before he walks into the adjoining bathroom, so I follow him, crossing my arms and bracing my hip on the door jamb while he takes a piss. Screw his privacy; I want to hear his explanation.

"If you don't get it, then just think about it," he says without looking at me. "What can I give you that a woman can't?"

"Huh?" I ask.

"With a man or a woman, you can fuck them both, right? But a woman can't very well fuck you, can she?" he points out. "Bisexual men, who are not happy in their heterosexual relationships, come to me because I have a cock and they want me to fuck them with it."

"Oh," I mutter in understanding.

"Gay men who have no interest in women, could want it either way, of course, but I've never let anyone fuck me," he says as he puts his dick in his boxer briefs and turns around to face me finally.

"And I've never even fucked a woman," I point out. "I don't know what it's like, but I know I want to do it."

"So what are you saying? That if I don't let you fuck me, you'll find someone who will?" Pax asks, his jaw ticking as he crosses his arms over his chest to match my stance.

"Yes. No. I don't know!" I reply, throwing my hands up in the air. "I'm tired of being a fucking virgin! I thought I could wait until I found a woman and was married or whatever, you know? But when we're together..."

"You want to fuck," Pax finishes.

"So damn bad," I tell him with a needy groan. "Could you imagine if you never had..."

"No," he says with a shake of his head while pinching his bottom lip between his finger and thumb as if in thought. "I seriously don't know how you've made it this long without fucking something."

"Me either. Maybe because I hadn't met anyone like you, you pushy bastard with your gay pornos and cock suckers and...and public blowjobs," I joke as I stroll up to Pax and reach around to fill both of my hands with his perfect, bubbly ass that I haven't been able to stop thinking about. "Even if I had my choice of any woman or you, I would still want you to be my first," I say, trying to butter him up with the truth.

I wait impatiently while Pax's dark chocolate eyes bore into mine for several long moments before he blows out a breath and says, "Fine."

"Fine?" I say again, unable to prevent my humongous smile.

"Yes, I'll try it once, but that's it," he tells me with a repeated poke to my bare chest. "There's no guarantees of anything else afterward."

"I'll take what I can get," I gladly agree. "So, we're both gonna pop our cherries together?" I ask, my dick already hard just thinking about it.

Glancing down between us at my growing length behind my fly and then lifting his head with his eyebrow arched, Pax says, "It's not happening right now, Moby Dick," bursting that little bubble.

"Then when?" I ask, hoping he's not procrastinating because he's gonna chicken out.

"Soon. There's prep involved," he explains while his fingertips glide over my chest and down my abs that tighten under the intimate caress. "You can't just stick it in."

"When?" I ask again as his hand lowers to the bulge in my jeans and cups it, causing my breath to stagger. "I need you, Pax."

"It'll be a surprise," he says. Slipping his hand down the front of my pants, he starts stroking me again. "For now, I'll let you fuck my mouth if you want –"

He barely gets the last word out before I grab his shoulders and push him down on his knees so I can start shoving my pants out of the way to free my cock.

Wrapping his hand around the base of my shaft, Pax looks up and asks, "Do you trust me?"

"Hell yes," I tell him, wetting my parted lips that have gone dry in anticipation.

"Seriously, do you trust me to try something? I agreed to trust you, so it's only fair..." he trails off and then leans forward, placing the head of my dick on his hot, wet tongue.

"Fuck, yes," I groan as my head falls back in ecstasy. Even though I just came a few minutes ago in his hand, I'm rearing and ready to go again. This time will still probably happen way too soon.

When his incredible mouth pulls away, I look down to see why he stopped and find Pax sucking on his finger.

"What are you..." I start to ask before he silences me, taking me deep into his mouth again and sucking the ever-loving shit out of me as he pulls back. Needing his head to bob faster, I thread my fingers through his hair and take control, thrusting my hips forward into his mouth as fast and deep as I need it until I'm completely lost to the pleasurable rhythm. So lost and so close to coming that I don't even tense up when Pax's fingertip presses against my back door. It's not exactly...unpleasant.

Even though I'm expecting it, there's a slight sting of surprise as he pushes his digit deeper, but as long as his mouth is on me, I don't care what the fuck he...

"*Ohfuckme,* I'm coming!" I yell as my entire body lurches forward so hard I have to catch myself on the sink when he presses his finger against something inside me that sends me soaring without any warning.

One hand braced on the counter, I use the other to grip Pax's head by his hair, pulling him toward my body as my shaft jerks with my release that shoots down his throat.

Only after my body stops shuddering does Pax remove his mouth or his finger from me, which is even more noticeable now.

Looking up at me with a knowing smirk while he swipes a hand over his mouth, he asks, "How was it?"

"Awful," I tease with a satisfied smile. "Didn't do anything for me."

"Liar," he says with a proud grin while still on his knees. "Admit it. You liked it."

"Maybe," I concede. "Don't you?"

"Yeah, but a little teasing is more than enough for me," he says, using the sink to pull himself back to his feet. "Now I need a shower, and then I'm gonna pass out."

When he goes over and turns the faucet on inside the walk-in shower, I realize how late it's getting and know I need to leave soon.

"Join me?" Pax asks, pulling out two fluffy towels from the closet and facing me, waiting for my decision. "You're gonna bail on shower time?" he says before I can reply. Still smiling, Pax turns around, takes off his shirt and then bottoms and steps into the flowing water, purposely flaunting his ass that I can't resist.

So I strip down and follow him inside, not for more orgasms but just to get a chance to soap up his long, lean frame. After I'm finished with him, I hand over the washcloth, and Pax washes every inch of me reverently, and I mean every inch. He spends twice as long as I did on him, making sure he doesn't miss a spot.

But then, when we're drying off, I know it's way past time for me to leave. Practice starts early tomorrow, and I have a captain's meeting even earlier. If I stay, then that'll mean waking Pax up at five a.m. when I have to get going.

"Go on, already," Pax grumbles as he leaves the bathroom in search of clean clothes in the bedroom and I'm putting on the ones I wore over. "You apparently have to go, and I need some sleep. Don't make a big deal out of it," he calls out.

Okay, so maybe he doesn't want me to stay as much as I wish I could.

"Fine," I mutter, now fully dressed and watching him run around the room, cleaning up the dirty clothes and towels. "See you tomorrow?" I ask since, on Friday nights, practice ends early. "I could stay all night," I offer.

"Probably not," he says without stopping the tidying. "I'm going to check out a club, so being that it's in public and all...I probably won't be home until late."

"Yeah, okay," I reply, understanding his meaning. Being seen alone together in public would be a mistake. Someone could snap a photo, and then I'll be the gay tight end. My career would be over. I would probably likely lose most of my friends, and my parents...I can't even consider dropping that type of bomb on them with everything else going on with my mom.

"See you whenever I guess," I say before I let myself out wondering how Pax and I could be so right and intimate in bed and then not even be capable of saying goodbye without becoming distant from one another.

CHAPTER 14

Pax

"I hope you don't mind, but I brought a few friends along," Roxy says with her usual peppy smile when we're standing outside of *Oxygen*, the hottest club on the Carolina coast with half of the starting Wildcats team looming behind her in their fancy duds.

"Oh, yeah. That's...yeah, that's great," I stammer in surprise.

"Ready to go inside?" Roxy asks, her smile faltering at my less than enthusiastic greeting to Kohen, Quinton, his cute little blond girlfriend Callie, Cameron, Nixon and, of course...Lathan. That's when I remind myself to quickly look away from him and avoid the tight end for the night for fear of giving away his secret. Our secret. Whatever.

"Sure, let's go," I agree, straightening my jacket as I turn around and lead the way to the door, hoping the fact that a plastic object is currently lodged in my ass isn't obvious when I walk.

I didn't tell Lathan, but all day I've been walking around with a butt plug, gradually increasing in size to prepare myself for him. Why did I wear it here tonight? Well, other than the fact that it takes time to ensure it won't be an unpleasant experience, I wanted the reminder of who was waiting for me.

It's no secret that I'm a notorious flirt. I don't even try, it just... happens. Maybe it's my friendly personality toward the same sex, but they always seem to know I'm gay, and they usually seem to think I'm coming on to them. Most of the time, if I'm not seeing anyone, then that's exactly what I'm doing. So tonight, I didn't want to let my flirting get out of hand when I have someone I want waiting for me.

Seeing him here, the flirting point is moot, yet that doesn't change the fact that I'm walking around stuffed. Now that sensation that's becoming more and more pleasant is a reminder of what the two of us are going to do hopefully soon. Maybe tonight? I know Lathan is getting impatient, and since I don't want him going somewhere else, especially to a woman, I'm ready to give this opportunity to him even though I'm nervous.

I never realized how much trust is involved when you bottom, which is probably why I've never let anyone else fuck me before now. There was no one I trusted like Lathan. He's a good guy, and I know he wouldn't screw me over. He may not be ready to come out now, or anytime in the near future, but at least he's honest about it rather than playing games.

When we get to the door, my name is already on the club's list tonight, along with one guest, so I ask the hostess to add six more, five of which are Wildcats players. Pics of them here will be priceless for the club's promotions on their website and social media, so I know it won't be a problem with Derrick, the manager. He'll probably kiss my ass for bringing them along.

I've been talking to Derrick about my club since I didn't want to come into town as backstabbing competition. He was nice enough to answer my questions about the sustainability of a business in this area and didn't seem the least bit concerned about me stealing his business since we plan to cater to two different demographics. In fact, he said to let him know if there was anything else he can help with and gave me a list of his vendors.

With the sweep of a pen, the hostess shows our group inside and seats us in one of the leather sofa, VIP sections with cocktail tables. A waitress promptly comes over and takes our drink order. Everyone orders alcohol except for Callie, who Roxy told me just recently became pregnant. The seven of us finally get situated; me on one end next to Roxy, then Kohen, Callie, Quinton, Cameron, Nixon, and Lathan on the far end, which is probably best. The further away he is, the less likely I can eye fuck him.

"This place is pretty crowded," Roxy leans over and shouts over the music into my ear. "Good sign since it's the offseason."

"Very true," I agree. "The local colleges and military bases around here help keep the city in business, unlike most of the other coastal towns."

That's right; I've done my research. Roxy and Lathan weren't the only reasons why I decided on Wilmington.

"Want to dance?" she asks.

"Ah, not at the moment," I reply as I look out onto the dance club. Leaning over, Roxy must ask Kohen if he wants to even though I can't hear her. He nods, and then the two of them are up and leaving.

Quinton and Callie follow them. And not long after that, the two wide receivers bet a hundred dollars on who can pick up a woman first before taking off toward the dance floor. That means only Lathan and me are left behind.

Now that there are no close witnesses, I let my eyes land on him, taking in his gray slacks fitted to his long, thick, muscular thighs and white dress shirt with the sleeves rolled up to his elbows. The outfit is so different from the usual athletic wear I see him in. Or the nude. He looks good. Very handsome and rich like the professional football player he is. And I'm not the only one who thinks so.

Two girls in short dresses, despite the cool temperature outside, saddle right up to him, each one practically humping his long legs spread wide when they lean over to talk to him. Unable to see much of Lathan, I can tell his lips are parted as he listens to them and blatantly checks out the tits spilling out in front of his eyes.

Yep, he's definitely straight. A gay man would be able to maintain eye contact.

Whatever the women ask, Lathan shakes his head, and then they sit on either side of him.

The sluts might as well have "easy three-some" signs hanging around their necks. Both place their fake nails on either of Lathan's thighs, and that's when I see the panic on his face when he glances over at me. I shrug and pick up the shot glass in front of me to throw it back in one gulp.

What the fuck does he expect me to do? Storm over and yank them up by their skanky heads of hair and say, *"Leave him alone; he's with me?"* Not fucking likely. I won't be the one who outs him. He would never forgive me.

So, I sit and watch from the corner of my eye as two women try and fuck Lathan right there in the middle of the club until I'm ready to explode.

...

Lathan

"Excuse me. I, ah, need to go to the restroom," I tell the girls draped all over me when I think of the one place where they can't follow me.

"We could go too if you want," one whispers into my ear, blowing that brilliant idea all to hell.

And knowing these two girls are both offering to let me fuck them should at least make my dick hard, but nope, nothing. Okay, well not *nothing*. There are four nice, big tits in my face, so my pants are a little snug, but not like when I think about being with Pax.

"That's okay. I'll be right back," I tell the ladies as I extract myself from their grasp and start for the dance floor in search of an escape.

When Quinton asked if I wanted to come with them to a club Pax was checking out, for whatever reason, I couldn't say no. I should've thought this through better since it doesn't matter if we're in the same room together or not. We can't even speak to each other without worrying someone will think we're...more. Pax has barely even looked in my direction, and...I fucking hate that.

A few fans recognize me on the way to the back of the club, asking for autographs that I quickly sign before quietly slipping away before they can ask for a selfie.

I find the men's room and have my dick in my hand pissing when I hear someone come in whistling the Jeopardy tone, making me smile.

"I shouldn't have come," I say before I even glance over my shoulder to see him.

"Why did you?" Pax asks, his tone conveying annoyance as he straightens his tie.

"Why do you think?" I ask rather than say I wanted to see him out loud in public.

Instead of coming to the urinal, Pax walks over to the stalls. I hear several doors bang open before he says, "It's empty..."

"And?" I ask even though I'm already zipping up my pants to go and join him.

"We can't stay in here long," I warn him as I step into the large, thankfully clean, stall and pull the door shut behind me.

As soon as I turn around, Pax is on me, kissing me so hard with his tongue in my mouth that my back hits the door. We grab and clutch at each other's clothes until we can't possibly get any closer. Well, not unless...

"I'm ready," Pax says as his mouth moves down to my neck.

"Okay," I say as my eyes close in bliss before his words penetrate my lust-hazed mind. "Oh! You're *ready* ready?" I ask.

"Yes, but not here," he tells me when his palm reaches down to squeeze my cock. "After."

"How long until after?" I ask impatiently, needing him. My knees are so weak that only the door is holding me up between the sensation of his wet mouth on me and his hand working me over.

"I need to talk to a few people, look around some, so say an hour? My place?" he asks when he pulls away, and I fight the urge to push him to his knees. He would do it if I asked, but he's right --- not here. Once we start, I don't want to stop until I'm inside him.

"Sure," I agree. "And you think you want to..."

"Yes," he says. Grabbing my hand, he places it on his ass, and I do the rest, squeezing, kneading my way to the place I'm dying to get in.

"Ughh fuck," Pax groans, his eyes rolling back in his head from the slight touch. Enjoying his reaction, I undo his belt to slip my hand down the back of his underwear where I quickly find the source of his moaning.

"What's this?" I ask, pushing on the plastic button.

"Getting...ready...for you," he gasps as I twist, push and pull on the device. "Shit! Stop before I come!"

"Just from that?" I ask in amazement that he's already so close.

"Remember my finger?" he reminds me.

"Oh, right. *That* spot," I say in understanding, unable to resist pressing the button deeper.

"Ugh, God. So. Close," he moans. "Stop, stop, stop."

"Fine," I reluctantly agree, only because I want him to come while I'm inside of him for the first time. *Both* of our first times. After waiting for so long, I know I'm ready now; and I'm so damn happy it will be with Pax.

"Fuck, I can't wait," I tell him, removing my hand out of his pants and kissing him. I tug on his bottom lip with my teeth when I pull away.

"Me too, which is...surprising," Pax says as he begins to fix the front of his shirt and redo his belt. Knowing he's not just on board for me but wants me to fuck him turns me on even more. I just hope I can make it good for him too and not let him down. That pressure causes a knot of anxiety in my gut.

"See you soon," I say with one last quick kiss before I open the door and slip out of the bathroom.

The sooner Pax finishes up here, the sooner I can finally lose my virginity. And it's about fucking time even if I am scared to death.

CHAPTER 15

Pax

After chatting with Derrick for the required amount of time, I quickly say my goodbyes to Roxy and the rest of the group so I can get home to Lathan. Am I nervous? Fuck yes. I'm doing something way out of my comfort zone, something I never thought I would do. I guess love can make you compromise.

What the fuck?!?

Stepping outside, the cold, coastal winter air smacks me in the face as I rewind my recent thoughts.

Did I just say *love*?

Do I love Lathan?

No, no way. It's too soon. We barely know each other, and all we do is screw around. I love his dick, sure. And the way he kisses me. He's so fucking hot it's unreal. But all of that has to do with lust, *not* love.

The two of us are sneaking around, and I have no clue if Lathan even wants more than to satisfy his curiosity tonight, get more experience, and then hit the road to find a nice woman to spend the rest of his life with. That's what bisexual men who play football do. They sure as fuck don't come out of the closet and marry their gay boyfriends in front of the entire world.

But I'm getting way ahead of myself, and if I don't rein it in, I'll end up ruining what could be one helluva night with Lathan.

The fact that he wants me to be his first has to mean something pretty significant. Lathan's made it this long without losing his virginity and is giving in to me. I should probably feel bad about leading him into temptation, but I don't. He made it clear that he wants to fuck me and is tired of waiting. He's ready, so I'm not going to try and talk him out of it, even if I should because he could end up regretting being with a man. Losing his virginity to me is not something he can ever take back once he's married with three kids, and his wife asks him about his first time...

When I pull up in front of my place, Lathan's Jeep is already there with the lights off, but he's still sitting inside. When I park, he gets out, and I meet him on the sidewalk.

"Hey," I say, knowing better than to touch him outside even if it is dark and there's likely no one within sight this time of night in the neighborhood.

"Hey," he says, his smile obvious in the moonlight.

"I was just asking myself on the way home if I should try and talk you out of this," I admit to him as we walk next to each other up the sidewalk to my front door.

"Fuck that," Lathan says. "You can't talk me out of it," he says in a rush. "Hold up. You're not having second thoughts, are you?" he grabs my shoulder to turn me to face him. "Because if you are, we don't have to..."

"I'm not having second thoughts," I assure him, wanting to reach for him but knowing better. "I want to do this. I just feel a little guilty that you'll be losing your virginity to me, and that's not something you can take back or redo. Once it's done, it's done."

"I know that Pax," Lathan replies. "Believe me; I get it. I'm not a fifteen-year-old naïve boy with a persistent hard-on who is determined to get laid at any cost. For years I've understood the consequences, the weight of this decision, and I know I won't ever have a single regret about tonight."

"You're sure?" I ask for the last time.

"One hundred and ten percent," he replies, leaning down to kiss me quickly before jerking away, remembering we're still on my porch and the moment isn't private. And, God, I hate that we can't just kiss each other whenever we want without fear.

Unlocking the door, I push it open for Lathan and then follow him inside.

"Bedroom?" he asks.

"Yes," I agree, not wanting to delay this moment any longer. With every step, the plug in my ass is a constant reminder of what's to come.

Instead of flipping on the blinding overhead lights in the bedroom, I walk around and turn on each of the bedside lamps to give the area a warmer, more intimate glow.

"Let me go get cleaned up, and I'll be right back," I tell Lathan before I shut myself in the adjoining bathroom. It's time to remove the plug and prep, neither of which are very romantic. And, fuck, I'm nervous. I don't think it's just about my vulnerability either. While we've fooled around plenty of times before, this is Lathan's first time truly sharing his body with another person, and that means something to me. Hell, it means a lot that he's giving his virginity to me.

Once I'm undressed and ready, I push down my nerves and open the door to the bedroom. Lathan is sitting at the foot of the bed, naked, with my big bottle of Grey Goose in his hands.

"Are you getting drunk?" I ask him indignantly, my worry morphing into anger. After the whole talk about how confident he was about doing this, needing to get shit-faced to do it isn't a very good sign that he meant it!

"No, not drunk," he answers with a shake of his head. "Just, taking the edge off."

"Fuck, Lathan," I grumble, shoving my fingers through the front of my hair and mussing it when I hate having a single hair out of place. That's how frustrated I am right now. "We shouldn't do this."

"This is what I want –" he starts.

"Then why can't you do it sober?" I snap at him.

"Because I'm...because I'm nervous, okay?" he replies, a blush coloring his cheeks. "Don't you remember your first time?"

"Oh," I mutter in comprehension. He's not having doubts about being with me. He's having performance anxiety.

I go over and take a seat next to him and steal the vodka bottle for a big swig before handing it back to him.

"I was seventeen my first time," I admit to him. "My parents had just kicked me out of the house and banished me to Tennessee to live with my Nana. In the middle of my junior year, I was starting at a new high school, and I made sure it was no secret that I was gay."

"Really?" Lathan asks before taking a long draw from the bottle. "You were brave enough to come out in high school?"

"Yeah, I was sick of hiding, but mostly I was so fucking horny. And I figured it would help my odds of finally getting some action if I made my preferences known."

"Did it?" he asks.

"Oh yeah," I reply with a grin, starting to feel the warmth of the alcohol in my veins. "Within a few weeks, Scott Howard, this senior who played guitar for a garage band, befriended me and asked me if I wanted to come listen to them play at his house. So, I did. And they sucked," I tell Lathan with a chuckle, remembering that my ears were nearly bleeding from the rhythmless commotion they were making. "But afterward, when everyone else was gone, we started making out on this old, blue plaid couch in the garage. That's where I got my first kiss, my first blowjob. And a few days later, Scott rode my dick in that same spot. I lasted all of three seconds before I came, but he didn't last much longer either, so..."

"What if I'm not good at it?" Lathan asks, getting to the root of the problem.

Standing up, I take the bottle from his hand and go over to set it on the bedside table. And then, when I'm back in front of Lathan, I grasp his face between my hands and bend down to kiss him, hard and long until the tension leaves his body and he relaxes. That's when I pull back and tell him, "You will be good. But even if you're not, I wouldn't know the difference," reminding him that this is all new to me too.

With a nod and a heavy exhale, Lathan gets to his feet, and we resume our kiss. Both of our cocks are ready and eager between our bodies, even if we're not.

Eventually, I make the first move, sitting down on the bed and pulling Lathan down with me, our tongues tangling as we crawl toward the head of the bed. When his mouth eases its way down my neck, I tell him, "There are condoms and lube in both nightstands."

Lathan nods in understanding but continues kissing his way over my chest and licking my nipple before taking it into his mouth. His teasing goes on for a while, only stopping when he reaches over to the drawer on the left to grab the supplies.

"Sit back on your knees," I tell him, taking the condom wrapper from him and opening it. I want to take care of our protection since I know Lathan doesn't have much experience with rubbers. He bites his bottom lip while I roll the latex down his rock-hard shaft and then slather it with lube.

"I'm ready if you are," I tell him since I applied lubrication to myself in the bathroom.

Leaning down, Lathan kisses me again, sweet and slowly this time. Neither of us gets in a rush, not until his hips begin to rock, anxious to find an opening. Pulling my knees to my chest and spreading them, I wait for Lathan to guide himself inside me for the very first time. Holding his shaft, he lines himself up. Gray eyes locked with mine, Lathan finally pushes forward. His lips part with a sudden gasp followed by a deep groan when the head of his cock eases into me. He's certainly thicker than the plug but causes only slight discomfort.

"You okay?" Lathan asks through clenched teeth.

"Yes, don't stop," I tell him, wanting to feel more of him.

With a sigh of relief, he pushes in deeper and doesn't stop until he's all the way in. Both of us shout explicatives, me because of the new, sudden fullness. Thankfully, Lathan doesn't move again right away, allowing me to have time to relax and get used to the unfamiliar feeling.

"So good," Lathan groans from above me before he pulls back and plunges into me. "Have to do that again," he says before he starts moving. I completely understand the primal urge. Once your dick is surrounded by the tight heat, instincts take over.

"That's it, baby. Fuck me," I encourage him, my own pleasure building with every one of his thrusts to my prostate. Reaching down, I start tugging on my cock as Lathan's years of contained control snaps. He pounds into me harder, each stroke hitting that wonderful spot, inching me closer to my release.

I come before him, my entire body tensing and clenching, nowhere more so than where Lathan fills me.

"Oh fuck!" he shouts, and I know firsthand how enjoyable that sensation is from his position.

Lathan slams forward one last time and his chest trembles above me as he experiences his first orgasm while being buried inside another person.

Lowering himself down until his face is concealed in the crook of my neck, he says, "Was I too rough? I sort of...lost it."

"No," I tell him, smoothing my palms up and down the hard muscles of his now sweaty back. "But I wouldn't have cared if you had been."

"Good...it was so good," he whispers with a kiss to my throat. "Thank you."

Before I can figure out how to respond to his sweet appreciation, Lathan asks, "Can I stay here tonight?"

"Sure, babe. Whatever you want," I say, glad he doesn't want to just run off after such an intimate experience.

"I don't have practice tomorrow," he explains. "But the plane for New York leaves at three."

"I'll make sure you're up in plenty of time," I promise him.

Still peppering me with kisses on my neck, he says between them, "We're not coming back until late Monday...and I'm going to stay with my parents Tuesday because we have a Thanksgiving game. I don't know when I'll see you again."

"That's okay," I assure him, rubbing my hands over his warm skin. "I know your schedule is hectic. And I've already told Nana I would fly back Wednesday to be with her for Thanksgiving."

"Oh," Lathan mutters, pulling back to look at me. "So you're not coming to Thursday's game?"

"Not this week," I answer. "If I don't go home, she'll be alone since my asshole parents never come over during the holidays anymore."

"So when will you be back?" he asks.

"I dunno. Friday or Saturday I guess." I gauge his reaction. "You're not gonna miss me, are you?" I tease.

"What? No, of course not," Lathan quickly replies before he climbs off of me. "I'm gonna go take a shower," he says before disappearing.

Lord give me patience. I know he's never been in a serious relationship, and he's probably never imagined himself in one with another man, but wow, he can still get so defensive at the drop of a hat. After something so amazing as our first time, it's like he suddenly has the emotional maturity of a teenager.

Just like all the others, I can't help but think to myself.

Most guys I've dated in the last few years only wanted to keep things light. It was just about having hot sex once in a while. Nothing else.

But Lathan's not like that. This is all new to him. He just has to get used to the idea of us being an actual couple for the first time in his life, learning the give and take. That's all. I'm sure it will take some time, but hopefully, he'll realize he wants more with me too, and that it's okay to tell me he cares about me and misses me.

When Lathan comes back from the shower, he barely says another word. He just climbs in bed and rolls over, so his back is to me. I curl up behind him, spooning him with my arm around his waist.

"I'll miss you next week, and I can't wait to see you when I get back," I tell him honestly with a kiss to his shoulder.

"Me too," Lathan murmurs softly before we both fall asleep.

And by the time I wake up Saturday morning, he's already gone...

CHAPTER 16

Lathan

"Where did you disappear to so early last night?" Quinton asks me with his crooked grin as he takes the seat next to me on the team's plane. "I looked over and saw two hotties all over you, and then you were gone."

"We had a threesome in the bathroom," I reply deadpan.

"No way! Seriously?" he exclaims, turning in his seat to face me.

"No, not seriously," I reply with a laugh.

"Popping your cherry with two girls would be one helluva way to take it down," he remarks, causing my cheeks to begin burning as I remember *exactly* how I popped my cherry last night. And then I immediately turned into some emotional chick afterward when I realized I wouldn't see Pax for a week. Just one week away from him and I fucking hated it. Even worse, I hate that he always seems to know all of my vulnerabilities before I do. I don't want him to think I'm weak or clingy. But the truth is I do miss him. I missed him before

I even left his apartment this morning. That knot in my stomach was there all night, knowing I would have to leave him soon and not having the slightest idea how to deal with the whirlwind of emotions all swirling inside of me after our first time.

"Do you miss Callie when we're on the road and she can't come?" I ask Quinton.

"Fuck yeah. Of course, I do," he admits. "Hell, I even miss her and Brady when I'm at practice all day. When they're not with me, it's like I'm missing a piece of myself, you know?"

"Yeah," I agree, glad to hear him confess that instead of giving it the tough guy brush off. "But, wait, is it different from how you miss your parents?" I ask since I hate that I see them so infrequently, especially knowing my mom's time is likely running out.

"Hmm," Quinton hums as he chews on his bottom lip in thought. "I never really thought about it, but yeah. I love my parents and all; I just don't miss them the same way. I can go days without talking to them or months without seeing them, and while it sucks, it also seems normal. If I don't get to hear Callie's voice after a few hours, I feel... off."

"So it's a different type of love?" I question.

"I think so," he replies. "With my parents, that unconditional type of love is always the same, a constant, consistent amount, you know? But with Callie and Brady, and even our tiny baby I haven't even met yet, it's like the love is a dependency that gets stronger each day."

Thinking that over, I try to summarize it. "How we love our parents is maxed out from the beginning and mutual, which is all we've ever known with them. And then when you fall in love with someone, it continuously builds. That's why it can be so devastating if it ends?"

"Pretty much, yeah," Quinton agrees with a nod. "So what's with your sudden interest in the philosophy of love?" he asks. "Have you met someone or something?"

"Maybe," I say with a smile because I can't begin to even try to force out the lie.

"Wow, no shit?" he asks. "When? Who is she?"

"It's, ah, really new so I don't want to make too big of a deal out of it yet," I tell him to hopefully cut off further questions.

"New or not, it must be pretty intense if you're already contemplating whether or not you love her," he points out.

For a second, I imagine telling my best friend that I had sex with a man last night and that I think I'm falling in love with him. I've never heard Quinton use a sexual slur or say a negative thing about gay men, but I still can't imagine he would approve. No, he'll probably wonder if I've had a crush on him the entire time we've been friends, which I haven't. And then he'll likely stop talking to me because things would be too awkward. We would play like shit on the field, and everyone would start to ask why Quinton can't complete a pass to his tight end and there goes my career.

Nope, not gonna happen.

While I have plenty of money saved, it's not limitless, and my mom's medical bills are not cheap now that my dad quit his job to stay home and take care of her. They lost their insurance, so I cover every expense.

If I lose my multi-million-dollar football contract, the money I have in the bank will quickly dwindle away, giving my mom even more reason to give up on her cancer treatments. That can't fucking happen, so maybe, for now, I should stay away from Pax to be safe.

Just the idea of not seeing him again leaves me feeling gutted, but I can't risk the consequences of the league finding out about us and booting me. There's too much at stake.

...

Pax

Around midnight Saturday when I still haven't heard from Lathan even though Roxy texted me they got there safely hours ago, I decided to send Lathan a text message to ask if he had a safe flight just to have something neutral to talk about. His response is two short words, **Yeah, thanks.**

I tell myself he's probably just tired and needs to get rest before the game tomorrow, so I don't say anything else until Sunday afternoon.

The Wildcats lose to the Trojans by one point when they fail to get a two-point conversion after a fourth quarter touchdown. A few hours later, I decide to send Lathan another message similar to the one I send to Roxy.

Sorry about the game ☹

Roxy is then immediately on the phone with me, bitching about the refs not calling any of the holds and venting about everything else that went wrong for an hour, but I don't hear a word back from Lathan.

I lie in bed Sunday night holding my phone and going through all the possible reasons he hasn't responded. His phone could've died. But then wouldn't a team with over fifty players have *someone* who would let them use their iPhone charger? Maybe he's upset about the loss and doesn't want to talk to anyone. Maybe he's tired and went to bed early...

Even with all those excuses, my mind keeps coming back around to one glaring explanation: He just doesn't want to talk to me.

What if I was right and he's already regretting losing his virginity to me? I shouldn't have given in to him Friday night. He obviously needed more time to come around to the idea of sleeping with a man, and I stupidly rushed him.

CHAPTER 17

Lathan

"Lathan!"

Quinton's booming voice startles me Tuesday after my shower. I'm already getting dressed at my locker, my thoughts miles away and focused on heading home to see my mom today.

"Hey, yeah? What's up?" I turn around and ask him.

"Have you got a minute? There's something I need to talk to you about...but only in the parking lot."

"Ah, sure. Okay. I'm almost ready," I say in a rush since I have no idea what my best friend has to say that he doesn't want all the other guys to hear.

With a solemn nod of his dark head, Quinton turns around and leaves.

Oh shit.

Does he know, about Pax and me? That I'm not...straight? If he does, will I be in some sort of trouble with the team?

Fuck.

Worst of all, will he treat me differently? Quinton's been one of my closest friends, one of my first friends after so many lonely years of getting picked on. God, that would be so fucking awful if he ends our friendship, especially since I've never even thought about any of the players in a sexual way and definitely not my friends. In fact, there's only ever been one man that I find myself wanting...

Slipping on my athletic shoes, I hustle out of the practice field locker room and into the parking lot. There stands Quinton with his back leaning against his white Land Cruiser; his arms crossed over his chest.

"Hey, everything okay?" I ask in concern.

"Yeah, yeah," he says as he lowers his arms and straightens.

Based on his continued frown, I brace myself for the worst with my approach.

"It's just, well, I wanted to let you know that I'm gonna ask Callie to marry me."

"Oh, wow!" I exclaim in surprise and relief that this isn't about Pax or me. "That's great! Congratulations," I tell him.

"Thanks," he says as we exchange a masculine embrace. When we separate, he says, "I'm a little nervous about what she'll say, you know, since we haven't been together long. But Callie trusted me enough to get her pregnant, so hopefully that means she wants a commitment..."

He's nervous she'll say no. That's why he looks so upset.

"You shouldn't worry. I'm positive she'll say yes," I try to assure him. And it's the truth. While Callie may try and act like she's not head over heels in love with Quinton, I can tell that she clearly is based on the way she looks at him when he's not looking. There's no way she'll turn him down.

"Thanks. I hope you're right," Quinton tells me with a small smile. "If she does say yes, I wanted to ask you if you would be my best man."

"Seriously?" I ask him in shock, and he nods in the affirmative.

"Of course I'll be your best man. Thank you. I don't know what to say."

"You've been one of my best friends since our rookie year, and I don't know what I would do without you on or off the field," he says, nearly choking me up at the unexpected words.

"Ditto," I tell him honestly. "Anything you need, let me know."

"I appreciate that, and I need to take you up on it sooner rather than later," he says while reaching into his pocket and pulling out a black ring box. "I bought Callie's diamond engagement ring, but I'm thinking of waiting until Christmas to ask her."

"Let's see it," I say.

He flips the box open, revealing a big, stunning diamond surrounded by smaller ones. The shimmer is so blinding in the midday sun that I need my sunglasses.

"Callie is gonna love it," I tell him since I can't imagine many women who wouldn't want something so beautiful.

"You think so?" Quinton asks.

"Definitely."

"Good," he says in relief. "The thing is, I don't want her to find it around the house. And if Kelsey finds it, she would probably tell Callie."

"Right," I agree.

"So, will you hold it for me?" he asks.

"Me? You want me to..."

"Yeah, I trust you, man." Shutting the lid of the box, he holds it out to me. "So what do you say? Keep it safe for me for a few weeks until I decide when to ask her?"

"Ah, yeah, sure," I tell him as I cautiously take the box. "Just for reference, if I lose it, how much will it cost to replace it?" I ask.

"Around a hundred and thirty," he informs me, causing me to release a long whistle.

"Whoa, okay. I won't lose it," I assure him.

"Thanks, Lathan. I owe you one," he says with a slap on my shoulder.

"Glad to help," I reply. "Well, I better get on the road. Traffic is probably gonna be a bitch."

"Heading home?" Quinton asks.

"Yeah, Dad's cooking Thanksgiving dinner tonight, so..."

"Tell your parents I said hello," he says, being familiar with them after meeting and talking to them after most games before this year. "How's your mom doing?"

"She's hanging in there," I respond, not wanting to get into the details of her refusal to continue chemo and radiation, the only thing that could keep her alive for longer than a few weeks.

"Have a good one, and I'll see you here Thursday," I say before starting toward my Jeep.

"You too!" Quinton calls back.

Fuck, now what am I gonna do with this expensive ring to make sure it's safe?

Figuring keeping it on me is the best choice since someone could break into my car, I slip it into the zipper pocket of my hoodie and hit the highway.

...

Pax

Lathan hasn't called or sent me any text messages since Saturday night. While I want to be calm and hope it's because he's busy getting ready for the Wildcats franchise's first ever Thanksgiving Day game, I can't help but worry that it's because of what we did Friday night.

God, now I feel like a fucking woman wondering if he liked it or not. Will he want to do it again? The most surprising thing is that *I* wouldn't mind bottoming for him again. It felt better than I expected, so Lathan had to have enjoyed himself too, right?

Or, he could be regretting losing his virginity to me instead of a woman.

I thought that, if I could be his first, maybe he would never feel the need to sleep with a chick to see what he's missing. Now, I can't help but think he'll still be curious to find out what all the fuss is about with pussy and want to give it a try.

After the busy holiday weekend, when I'm in Tennessee visiting my Nana and he's making football history, everything will settle down, and I can talk to Lathan about us being...more.

Would he come out to really be with me?

His career could take a huge hit; I get that. So if he told me he wanted to be with me and that the league and public opinion were the only things holding him back, then I would wait. It's not like Lathan will play football forever; just a few more years. Years of sneaking around after I promised myself I was done with that shit...

The difference was, Oliver never had any intention of leaving his wife. He lied to me, and I know I can trust Lathan to be honest.

So, I just need to be patient over the next few days, not look at my phone every two seconds to check for a text message and see what happens.

These feelings I have about Lathan, well, they can't possibly be one-sided. Every night that we've been together it's felt too good and perfect for me to be wrong about him.

CHAPTER 18

Lathan

"Mom? Dad? I'm home," I call out after I unlock the front door of my childhood home with my key and step inside. My parents both worked when I was growing up, my dad moving up the ladder at the local bank, and my mom as a paralegal. So, while our house isn't huge, it was always a perfect, two-story size for the three of us. Once I went to the pros, I offered to buy them a bigger place, even one in Wilmington, but they wouldn't take my money. Well, not until my mom got sick and my dad had to quit his job to take care of her. They didn't really want to accept my help then, but I was able to convince them it was what was best for Mom without having to dip into their retirement funds.

No matter how long it's been, this place always smells the same when I walk inside, like the comforting scent of clean linens and vanilla. Those smells will always remind me of the happy place where I was raised with a wonderful mother and father.

Today, the house also smells like turkey and other delicious food.

"In the kitchen!" my dad calls out, so I start that way through the silent, empty living room.

"Hey," I say when I find him in his white apron, stirring whatever is cooking in the big pot on the stove. His short brown hair is even grayer than the last time I saw him just a few short weeks ago, and he looks leaner. If my mom's sickness has been hell on me, then I can't imagine what he's been going through.

"Hey there, son," he replies with a smile over his shoulder. Setting down his big spoon on the counter, he turns around and wraps me in a hug. My dad's a big man, but I outgrew him by a few inches that I used to love to tease about. The last few months there hasn't been any teasing or jokes, just the solemnness of dealing with cancer. "Good to see you. Your mom will be so happy you're here."

"I wish I could be here Thursday instead," I tell him as we embrace.

"What? No!" he scoffs after we separate. "Playing ball on Thanksgiving Day is incredible, Lathan! You should be proud of your accomplishment. All those years we've watched games together on TV, and now you're going to be out there on the field doing it!"

"Yeah, I am proud. It's just going to be weird not being home..."

"You're home now," he says. "That's all that matters. Besides, your mom sleeps so much her days are blurring together. She won't know the difference."

Fuck.

"Is she awake?" I ask, anxious to see her, but at the same time dreading it, knowing she's likely thinner and paler than the last time.

"No, she just went back to bed," he says with a sigh. "But she told us to go ahead and eat, and then you can tell her what all you've been up to lately when she gets up later."

"We can wait to eat," I suggest.

"No, your mother insisted we eat while it's hot and that she'll catch up with us," my dad says, leaving no room for argument.

The two of us pile food on our plates and sit down at the table to eat in silence. Seeing mom's empty chair makes my appetite disappear, but I don't want to hurt my dad's feelings. I make myself scarf down everything on my plate and even go back for seconds.

An hour and a half later after the leftovers have been put away and the kitchen is clean, my mom finally shuffles into the living room where my dad and I are watching the news. We both jump up from our seats to help her.

"Why didn't you call for me? I would've helped you out of bed," Dad asks her.

"Ah, I'm fine. Our sweet boy is home now, so I'm better than fine," she tells him before turning to me. I ease my arms gently around her frail back as she hugs my waist, and cringe when I feel how bony her body is. "So glad you're here, Lathan."

"Me too," I tell her, trying to swallow down the tears threatening to spill.

"Wait," she says when I reluctantly start to pull away.

"What's wrong?" I ask.

"What's that in your pocket?" she asks, patting the front of my hoodie.

"Oh, that," I say as I tug down the zipper and retrieve the ring box. "It's an engagement ring..."

"Oh my God!" she exclaims. "You've met a girl! Eddie, did you hear that? Lathan's met a girl, and he's gonna marry her!"

"That's not –" I start to say, but then she's hugging me so tight and crying on my chest.

"I knew my time wasn't up yet! I have to see my baby get married and have his own babies..."

"Mom..." I say with a sigh. But then my father's arms are around both of us, and the two of them are crying tears of joy. My mom because she thinks I've found someone to love, and my dad probably because Mom's talking about the future rather than the end.

How can I possibly tell them the truth now that the ring is Quinton's and intended for *his* future wife?

And honestly, there's nothing I wouldn't do to keep my mom alive and happy...

The last few months she's started to give up, to accept her fate. When she was first diagnosed over a year ago, she had the spirit of a fighter. Over time, through the sickness and the side effects of all the various treatments, she's grown weary. Maybe me getting married will be enough to encourage her not to throw in the towel just yet. With continued chemo and radiation, it's possible that she could eventually put the cancer in remission.

So, I take a deep breath and decide to tell a little fib.

"Yes, I met someone," I say, which after I say it I realize it's the truth.

"Why didn't you tell us?" Mom asks me while still gripping my upper arms, a bigger smile on her face than I've seen in a long time.

Yes, why didn't I tell my parents I met someone that I planned to marry? Think fast, Lathan! Think fucking fast!

"I just...I didn't want to get too excited and tell everyone in case she says no," I lie.

"What? That's impossible!" my mom declares. "Any girl would be so lucky to have you!"

Any girl? Hell, I would be happy with just one imaginary girl at this particular moment. What the fuck am I gonna do? Place an ad in the paper that says, *WIFE WANTED*? Get on the internet and find one of those mail order brides?

One problem at a time. For now, I just have to put off giving them any particular name or specific details.

"I don't really want to talk about her and jinx it," I tell them. "If she says yes, then I'll let you meet her right away."

"When are you going to pop the question?" my dad questions.

"Soon," I say, although that depends entirely on how fast I can find a single woman to agree to marry me.

Time is running out for my mother, so I can't afford to be picky. After Thursday's game, I'll find someone to marry me, even if I have to pay them to pretend they care for me.

And then, there's Pax...

How the fuck can I tell him that I'm looking for a wife without him losing his shit?

For years I told myself that I would find a nice girl and save my virginity until we got married. Instead, Friday night I couldn't resist, and so my first time was with a man. Do I regret it? Hell no. Being with Pax was so damn amazing that I hate we waited as long as we did. Even before that night, when I thought about my first time, I wanted it to be with Pax.

Why I've always been so shy and awkward around women seems so obvious now --- I may have been attracted to them, but I just didn't really want them. I thought asking girls out and being with them was what I was *supposed* to do. And while I may get turned on by a woman's naked body, the desire to sleep with one has never really been there. If it had been, I would've tried harder, given into any number of the solicitations I've received from women since I became a professional football player.

After being with Pax, there's not even the least bit of curiosity about hetero sex left in me. I don't want a woman. I want Pax.

But more than him, I want to give this incredible milestone to my mother while I still can. Coming out to my parents, my friends, my team would be too hard, not just on me, but it could devastate my mom, who is already in a fragile state. I could lose my friends that I have for the first time in my life. And by causing problems and conflict with the other players, it would ruin the rest of our season that's already started out rocky.

I have to do the unselfish thing, which is to not come out of the closet right now but do this for my mother. Getting married to a woman would even quash any rumors that could surface about Pax and me, so it's sort of perfect timing there too.

I bet Pax would even understand. Well, probably not the wedding part, but that I'm not ready to sacrifice everything for our relationship that is so new. That means I'll have to tell him what I plan to do and hope that he cares enough about me to wait for me to see it through.

CHAPTER 19

Pax

"There he is, Nana," I tell my grandmother after she cooked the full Thanksgiving spread for just the two of us and we sit down to watch the Wildcats game on her old tube television. It's not that she can't afford a flat screen, because she's loaded. The woman's just stingy, which is how her and my grandfather saved so much money.

My parents are invited to join us every year, yet they never show up; and neither Nana nor I care.

"Which one?" she asks, scooting up on the edge of her recliner to get a closer look through her thick glasses.

"Number eighty-six," I tell her, going up to the fuzzy screen and pointing to Lathan as he runs down the field and catches a pass.

"He's got a nice butt," she replies, making me laugh out loud.

"Yeah, he does," I agree as I retake my seat on the sofa to watch the game.

"Is he the girl or the guy?" Nana asks, not the least bit shy asking me about my sex life.

"Well, I guess you could say he's the guy," I admit. "Although, I would like to convince him to be the girl one of these days."

Cackling, she slaps her knee and says, "Heavens to Betsy! I thought you were always the guy."

"We're crossing into TMI territory, Nana, so let's draw the line right there, shall we?" I ask her.

Telling my grandma about my relationships is nothing new. And Lathan doesn't have to worry about her outing him since she's old school. She doesn't have any internet, her phone only dials locally, and none of her friends can hear worth a shit. If she told them "Lathan Savage is gay", none of them would know who the fuck he is, and they would probably think she said, "Looks like we'll have to scavenge until May."

What I don't tell Nana is that I haven't talked to Lathan since the night he popped my cherry, and it's freaking me out a little.

Tomorrow, I'm headed back to Wilmington. And if I still haven't gotten a message from him, I'll show up at his place and ask him point blank if we're done because fucking me was too gay for him.

Or maybe I'll wait a few more days, because the thought of us being over is too much to bear. Having him tell me that to my face is unimaginable.

...

Lathan

After we win our Thanksgiving game, Quinton invites everyone to a get-together at his house since most of the team has family out of state they can't be with today.

I would rather be with Pax, but he told me the other night he was going to Tennessee to be with his grandma, so here I am.

When I pull up in the crowded driveway, I see Kelsey, Quinton's babysitter, standing out front, bundled up in her black peacoat, the hood of her little blue Toyota up while she stares down at the engine.

Parking off to the side of the road, I get out and ask, "Hey, Kelsey. Having car problems?" as I approach.

"Oh, hi, Lathan! And, ugh, yes," the cute brunette says, flashing me a small smile. "I think it might be the battery."

"Well, then let me try jump starting it for you," I suggest.

"That would be great!" Kelsey says. "I was just about to go back inside to see if someone had any of those cable things or whatever."

"Just a second," I tell her.

Walking back to my Jeep, I crank it and drive it around in the grass so that it's close enough to her hood to connect the jumper cables I always keep on hand for emergencies like this. Once I climb out and clamp them in place on the terminals, I tell her to try the engine.

Kelsey sits down in the driver seat, and her car cranks right away.

"Yay! Thank you so much, Lathan!" she exclaims as she jumps out of the front seat and comes around to hug me. Tightly. And for a *lonnng* time. "Sorry, you smell so good," she says when she finally releases me, a goofy smile on her face. "I owe you big time."

"No, that's..." I begin to say it's okay when I turn around to unhook the jumper cables, and then I remember that I *do* need something in particular. Something huge that maybe she can help me with.

After stowing away the jumper cables under my backseat, I turn to her and ask, "Kelsey, are you seeing anyone, like, you know, dating anybody?" while looking at her more closely. She's young, maybe twenty-one or twenty-two, smart, sweet, and classically pretty with a fair complexion and dark hair and eyes. Quinton and Callie trust her implicitly with Brady. She's the fun-loving, optimistic type of girl that I know my parents would love.

"Um, no, I'm not," she answers, pushing her long brown hair behind one of her ears shyly.

"This is going to sound crazy, but I have a good reason for asking," I start. Slamming her hood back down, I rest my hip against the front of the car while I face her, trying to figure out how to come out and ask for what I need. I figure straight to the point is best, so I say, "Would you want to maybe marry me?"

"Huh?" she asks with her jaw falling open. After a moment, she recovers and says, "Did you just..."

"You see, my mom is...really sick, and Quinton gave me this ring to hold for Callie, but don't tell her," I explain as I pull out the ring box from my hoodie pocket and show to her. "My mom found it the other day and assumed I was getting married. And if it means she'll keep getting chemo and radiation treatments to prolong her life instead of giving up, I'm willing to do whatever it takes, including getting married..."

"Huh?" Kelsey asks again, blinking at me in confusion.

"Feel free to say no," I tell her. "This is an enormous favor to ask, especially since you don't know me very well, but would you consider doing this? Oh, and I can pay you. Just name your price."

"You-you're serious?" she asks with wide, confused brown eyes. "You're not screwing with me?"

"No, definitely not," I reply with a shake of my head. "I'm very serious and sort of on a deadline."

"I thought you were gonna ask me out, and you asked me to... to..."

"Marry me," I repeat with a wince.

"Right. That," she says, wrapping her arms around herself to keep warm. "Like for real?"

"Yes. And I'll pay you since I know this is a lot to ask of someone," I explain. "Maybe we can agree to a weekly rate, if that sounds fair? Although, I hope we're together for a lot of weeks if the treatments work this time. But don't worry. I have plenty of money. Oh, and you would probably need to move in with me, so there's that too. My townhouse has plenty of room, and it's close by," I continue rambling, pointing over my shoulder to the right where my place is. "If you need to think about it for a few days or whatever that's fine. There's just...not a lot of time left."

Placing her palm on my chest to stop my long-winded plea, Kelsey looks up at me with a smile and says, "Lathan, you don't have to pay me to be your wife. I would do that for free, for however long."

"Really? You would?" I ask again, my big gust of a relieved breath creating a cloud in the cold air between us. "Are you sure?"

"Absolutely," she says with a nod, her brown doe eyes watering. "That's the sweetest thing I've ever heard, and I would be happy to help you and your family any way I can."

"Oh my God. Thank you! Thank you so freaking much!" I tell her, giving her another hug that she doesn't seem to mind since she eagerly returns it.

"We're gonna get married. I'm getting married. Holy shit," she mutters against my chest.

Letting her go, I say, "How about I have an attorney, like, draw up papers, you know, a prenup or whatever? No offense or anything."

"Sure, of course," she agrees.

"And, ah, the wedding, it needs to happen soon..." I tell her with a cringe, adding to the enormous request. "That okay?"

"Soon. Yes, okay. Just give me a date," Kelsey replies happily.

"Could you handle making all of the arrangements?" I ask. "I'll pay for them. You can have whatever you want, as big and extravagant, just as long as it's in Elon where my parents live since my mom's not able to travel far."

"Yeah, sure. I can do that. I have plenty of time while Brady is napping every day."

"Wow, that's great. Thank you," I tell her again. "I'll leave a check with the attorney and call you to give you his address and all. And, well, I guess I need to get your phone number since you're going to be my wife and all," I say with a grin.

"Right," she says, returning my smile. "Let me grab my phone."

"How much do you think a wedding costs?" I ask as she leans inside the front of her car.

"Ah, I'm pretty money savvy, so I think...twenty thousand would cover everything for a really nice wedding and reception."

"Done," I agree, since that amount of money is nothing to me.

"Great," she says, and then we exchange numbers, punching them into our phones while our fingers nearly freeze off.

"So, um, how do you think we should tell everyone else?" I ask when that's done, nodding toward Quinton's house. "You know, without them suspecting something since it's all so sudden? I don't want *anyone* to know we made this arrangement, because it could get back to my mom..."

"I won't say a word," Kelsey holds up her palm to assure me. "And we could just act like we've been sneaking around for a few weeks because you thought Quinton might be upset since I work for him and all," Kelsey suggests with a shrug.

"Yes, that's a great idea," I agree, unable to believe how this is all coming together so easily. Just two days ago I didn't have a clue what I was going to do about finding a pretend wife, and now it's thankfully settled.

"All we have to do now is just...get caught," she says with a huge grin.

"Get caught. How do we do that?" I ask.

"Hmm, well, I have an idea if you can play along and don't mind kissing me," she replies with a tilt of her head.

"Kissing. I can handle kissing," I reply, more confident about those skills after practicing so much with Pax recently.

"We should get comfortable doing that together since we'll be expected to kiss a lot as an engaged couple," Kelsey says.

"That's probably a good idea," I agree.

"Okay. So, should we start now?" she asks.

"Now?" I repeat in surprise, my eyebrows shooting up in shock. "You want to start kissing right now?" I ask.

"I know you're shy, but it will be fine, Lathan. Come on, follow me and play along," Kelsey says as she goes over to the driver side of her car and sits down inside. "Ready?" she calls out since I haven't moved from the front hood of her car.

Kelsey is doing me a huge favor, so the least I can do is make this whole situation look legit by kissing her. She's sweet and pretty. I know how to kiss just fine now, so why does the idea of putting my lips on hers make me so fucking nervous?

Because I'll be cheating on Pax.

But it's not really cheating if it's a fake relationship, right?

Besides, it's not like I would ever feel Kelsey up or sleep with her. And if I don't enjoy kissing her, then it's not cheating. It's like...a job. Something I have to do as part of our pretend marriage to make my sick mother happy.

Taking a deep breath to calm my worries and nerves, I walk around to the open driver side door and tell her, "Ready," but still not completely sure what her plan is.

Kelsey reaches up and grabs the front of my hoodie and pulls my mouth down to meet hers. Not sure what to do with my hands, I put them where I would if she were Pax, slipping my fingers through her hair and gripping her neck. It must be the right thing to do because she moans softly against my lips.

Our kiss is...nice, but it doesn't turn me on like when I kiss Pax. There's nothing at all going on down below in my pants.

And, God, I can't wait to see Pax again...

Fuck.

Maybe I shouldn't tell Pax about this. What will he say about me getting married? I have a feeling that won't go over well.

I don't have any more time to dwell on that problem, because Kelsey presses her palm down on the car horn, making it blare into the quiet afternoon, definitely attracting attention before she grabs my shoulder to pull me closer to her.

"What the hell?"

Through the corner of my eye out the front windshield, I see

Quinton shouting when he steps out on the porch, followed by Callie holding Brady, along with Kohen, Roxy and our teammates, Nixon and Cam.

"Give me the ring," Kelsey whispers between pants like she's been running up the steps of the stadium.

Before I can move, she reaches into my coat pocket, pulls out the ring box, pops it open and then frees the diamond ring to slide it quickly onto her finger.

"Let's do this," she says to me with a smile, tossing the now empty ring box over her shoulder.

I stand up straight next to the car and wave to everyone watching. "Kelsey and I have some news!" I shout.

Offering her my hand, I pull her out of the car, and say, "We've been seeing each other for some time now, but I wasn't sure how Callie and Quinton would react, so we kept it a secret."

Everyone stares silently at us with wide eyes and slack jaws.

"The truth is, we're getting married. Soon because...we can't wait any longer," I tell them all.

"What?"

"Oh, my God. Seriously?"

"No fucking way!"

Their reactions are all pretty much the same, and I begin to worry that they're not buying it. But then, Roxy rushes down the front stairs and says, "Let me see the ring!"

Kelsey proudly holds her left hand out, showing off the ring Quinton bought for Callie.

Fuck. He's so gonna kill me for this.

Guess I should add *buy another engagement ring to replace the one Kelsey is wearing* to the top of my wedding to do list.

I'm getting married.

To a woman.

Which is insane since I'm in love with a man.

Wait, did I just say *in love*?

Yep, I love Pax, and I wish I could be announcing that the two of us are together, but that will never happen. I would lose my friends, the league could kick me out, and my parents would be devastated.

No. Despite how much I want Pax, we couldn't ever be like a real couple.

CHAPTER 20

Pax

Tell me when you get home. I need to see you.

I nearly fall out on the floor in relief when I got off the plane and turn on my phone to see that text message from Lathan.

He wants to see me.

No, he said he *needs* to see me.

Finally!

I consider replying with something snarky, pointing out that while he wasn't able to send me even a Happy Thanksgiving text when I was away, now he can't wait to see me since I'm back in town and we can fuck around. But I don't. That sounds like something a nagging girlfriend would do, and I am not the girl in this relationship. Well, not all of the time.

Is that all Lathan wants tonight? To come over and fuck me?

My cock lengthens down the leg of my suit pants at the thought.

Sure, I'll probably let him, but I better at least get a blowjob out of it.

Finally getting to my car at the airport lot, I toss my luggage into the trunk of my BMW and then sit down in the driver seat to reply to Lathan's message.

On my way home from the airport now. Meet me there?

I almost delete it since it sounds so desperate, but that's how I feel after not seeing or talking to Lathan for a week. Sad but true.

When I pull up at my place, Lathan is already out of his Jeep and waiting at the door.

Leaving my luggage to haul in later, I walk up the sidewalk to see my boy instead.

"Hey," I say with my approach.

"Hey," he replies before shoving his hands into the front pockets of his jeans. "I missed you."

"I missed you too," I reply, loving that he admitted that to me and barely refraining from throwing myself at him. When Lathan glances around the neighborhood, I know that wouldn't go over well, so I hurry up and unlock the door. "Guess you've been too busy to even –"

That's all the words I get out before Lathan attacks me, slamming me against the wall next to the door and kissing me violently. Not that I'm complaining. Instead, I reach for his hair and tug him closer with one hand while the other goes around to grab his ass, letting my fingers dip into the crease.

I don't even have time to ask for a blowjob before Lathan's mouth moves down my neck and his hands get to work undoing my pants. Going to his knees at the same time he jerks my boxer briefs and pants down, he inhales my cock like a starving man, sucking me deeper into his throat than ever before.

"Easy," I tell him between gasps. "Easy or...I won't...last. Oh, fuck!" I exclaim when Lathan pulls his mouth off my dick and moves lower to nuzzle my balls. He looks up at me with desire filling his stormy gray eyes as he eagerly devours each of them, licking and sucking so good, so desperately, like he can't get enough.

I have a moment of short reprieve when he shoves two fingers into his mouth and sucks on them before reaching between my legs and...

"God...damn," I groan to the ceiling when he simultaneously prods my puckered hole and starts sucking my dick again. He's a fast learner, remembering how I got him off.

My eyes close as he works one finger inside me and then two, all while his mouth brings me closer and closer to a release.

"Uhh fuck! Fuck!" I scream when his fingers hit my prostate, setting me off like a rocket. "So good. So good," I chant as I grip the sides of his head to ride out the waves.

Releasing my cock from his mouth, Lathan says, "Turn around," while still on his knees. My feet begin moving with my pants still around my ankles before I even command them.

Bracing my palms against the wall to hold myself up, Lathan grasps my ass cheeks in each of his hands and spreads them. I'm not even close to being prepared for the amazing sensations of his tongue flickering over that tight ring of muscles.

"Oh, God, that's...that's...*ahh,*" I moan through the bliss, his licking and prodding turning me into a puddle of need. That's why when Lathan stands up and thrusts his cock into me there's only a slight sting before the euphoria overwhelms it.

"Missed...this...ass," Lathan growls as he slams into me. "Need it," he says, grabbing the back of my hair to turn my head so his mouth can latch over my neck. His teeth dig into my skin while he invades me.

This time is so much different than our first, not better or worse. It's just, last Friday night, Lathan was so gentle and sweet. Unsure. I don't know what's gotten into him today, but the new confidence and aggressive side is hot too.

"Give it to me!" I encourage him. "Everything. Give it...give me..." I come again, spraying the wall in cum as Lathan grunts through his release and his hips pound into me so hard we may leave a permanent dent in the drywall.

"Not enough," Lathan says, but I'm still floating on the clouds to even try and decipher his meaning.

For several long minutes, neither of us move, not until his cock goes limp and slips out of me, right along with his hot, sticky release dripping down my ass cheeks and the inside of my thighs. The sensation itself isn't what bothers me; it's all the other possible consequences. That and maybe I'm still pissed that he's only spoken two words to me for an entire week, yet here he is fucking me again.

"You didn't use a condom?" I ask without turning around, even though it's obvious.

"Ah, no. I...I forgot."

"That's not something you fucking forget!" I yell at him while reaching down to pull my pants and boxer briefs back up. Once I'm covered again, I turn to face him.

"I'm sorry," Lathan says, his eyes lowered while shoving his cock back into the front of his jeans. "But you know you're the only one I've been with."

"The problem is that you have no way to know if you're the only man *I've* been with," I remind him. "The condom is just as much for you as it is for me."

Hands pausing on his jeans button, Lathan looks up with eyes wide. "Are you saying you let someone fuck you in Tennessee?"

"No," I respond on a huff. "I haven't let anyone but you fuck me and I get tested every few months. Still, you can't be too careful." Wanting to see his reaction to the idea of other men, I add, "And the next man you're with may not be clean."

Both of Lathan's blond eyebrows shoot up. "Next man?" he repeats. "What the fuck are you talking about?"

"We haven't said we're exclusive, so..."

"So what?" he snaps at me, his face turning red. "Are *you* planning to fuck other men on the side?"

"No," I assure him, scrubbing my fingers through my hair. "I was just saying we haven't talked about it, so I didn't know."

"Well, I don't want to see anyone else," he tells me, lifting the heavy anvil from my chest.

"Good. I don't either," I admit. "But I just don't know how this is all gonna work with you being in the closet."

"I can't be outed right now," he says immediately. "So this is all I can do. Take it or leave it."

"That's what I figured," I reply. "And I can wait if you tell me you're serious about us, that it's more than you fucking around whenever you want just because you're curious."

"You'll wait?" he asks. "Until I'm ready?"

"Yeah."

"What if it takes years?"

"Then you better make it worth my while," I reply with a grin. "And not fucking ignore me again for an entire week."

"I won't ignore you again," he quickly agrees. "And if you'll wait, give me the time I need, then I'll..."

"You'll what?" I ask when he pauses; his stormy eyes lowered to the carpet.

"I'll let you fuck me," he mutters.

"No," I reply without hesitation even if that's what I want more than anything.

"What? You don't want me anymore?" he asks, his forehead creased in confusion as he looks up to study my face for an explanation.

"Oh, I want you, so fucking bad," I assure him. "But not when having you is just a bargaining chip. I don't want to fuck you unless it's what you want."

"I do want it," he says softly. "I just couldn't admit it to myself or anyone else, because then it will really make me –"

"Don't say it," I interrupt, slapping my palm over his mouth. "It doesn't make you *anything* or change who you are. This is just between you and me, that's all it is. So don't even think about labels or whatever the fuck it is you're worried about."

Wrapping his hand around my wrist, he pulls my palm from his lips. "But what if I...what if I don't like it?" he asks. "Does that mean that we're over?"

"No," I promise him. "I'm not asking you to do this. Ever. Do I want to? Yes. Do I have to do it to still want to be with you? Absolutely not."

And fuck, if that's not a revelation; because the moment I say the words, I know they're true. Lathan's the only person I would ever agree to keep seeing even with fucking him off the table. I want him, however I can have him, so the sacrifice would be worth it.

"Good," Lathan says with what sounds like relief. "Then I want to try."

"You're sure?" I ask.

He nods before he speaks. "Yes. Tonight."

"We don't have to rush into –"

Lathan ends my sentence by grabbing me by the back of my neck and slanting his lips over mine. When he pulls away from our kiss, he says, "Pax, I want you to fuck me. Right now."

With a groan, I grab his hand and pull him into the bathroom where I start running warm water in my big garden tub. From underneath the sink cabinet, I pull out the condoms and lube and set them within reach on the tub rim.

"Here?" Lathan asks as I pull out two towels from the closet and then check the temperature of the faucet again with my hand.

"Here," I reply. "We can clean up, prep you, and fuck all in one convenient place. Now get naked."

"Yes, sir," Lathan says with a small smile that doesn't reach his eyes.

He's nervous. Fuck, I totally get it since I was in his shoes just a few days ago. It's scary to trust someone enough to let them in, and I'm ecstatic that he's giving this part of himself to me.

"Will it hurt?" he asks while taking off his clothes.

"Not as much as it will feel good," I tell him honestly before squeezing body wash into the running faucet to add suds to the bath water. After that's taken care of, I start removing my dress shirt and slacks. "Great game yesterday, by the way," I say as we watch each other get naked. "You were on fire, and my Nana said you had a nice ass."

"No, she didn't!" he challenges with a grin.

"She most certainly did," I reply.

Lathan chuckles, and I expect him to be upset that I told someone about us, but instead, he just says, "I guess you're about to find out just how nice my ass is."

Kicking my last leg free of my pants, I climb over into the tub and tell him, "Get in before I fuck you on the counter."

Still grinning, he follows me in. And after I take a seat with my back against one of the walls, Lathan lowers himself down on top of me, straddling my legs with both of his arms draped around the back of my neck. Our chests are pressed together as the warm, sudsy water rises, his ass is sitting on my dick, and I can feel his hard cock digging into my stomach.

This tub is turning out to be my favorite place in the world, and we haven't even had sex in it yet.

"Before we get too far gone," I start telling Lathan, so close our noses are brushing. "If you get uncomfortable or want to stop, just say so. Okay?"

"Okay," he agrees before brushing his lips lightly over mine. "First, I've been wondering..." he says. "I should've asked first before I... you know...again. Did *you* like it when I..."

Knowing exactly what he's referring to, I tell him, "Fuck, yes. More than I expected. Both times."

"Enough to want to let me fuck you regularly?" he asks, his thick shaft between our bodies growing harder with his obvious arousal.

"Oh, yeah," I agree. "I think I'm starting to see the appeal of switch-hitting," I tell him. "After I fuck you, you can fuck me; and if you like it, on and on it goes until we're both exhausted, limp dick bastards."

"Something to look forward to," he replies.

Reaching around to grab his ass and then tease his tight hole long enough that his jaw goes slack and his eyelids grow heavy, I tell him, "If you don't beg me to fuck you again, I'll be surprised."

Pushing my middle finger deeper, past the tight ring of muscles, I hit the spot that makes Lathan gasp loudly followed by a full-body shudder. There's no need for me to even ask him how it feels when he begins grinding down on my pumping finger, silently asking for more.

So, I give it to him, fucking him with one finger then two, scissoring them apart to get him ready to take me.

When he starts breathing so heavily I worry he's gonna hyperventilate, I tell him, "Turn around, face the mirror, and hold on to the tub rim."

Nodding without further comment, Lathan scrambles off of me and splashes around in the water to get into position. I want to do this from behind his first time to make it easier on him. With him facing the full-length mirror I can still watch his face to see his reaction.

When he's ready, I shut off the water; because if the tub gets any fuller, we'll be sloshing it over the edge. Then I stand up to open the condom and roll it on my achingly hard cock. Squirting some lube into my hand, I rub it up and down my latex-covered length before getting another handful. Kneeling down behind Lathan, I reach just under the water's surface and coat his opening, now able to slip three fingers inside him.

"*Fuuuuck.* Just do it already," Lathan urges.

Needing no further encouragement, I fist my cock and line it up. Pressing forward, I ease my swollen head in. It's nearly impossible to stop watching myself entering him, but I raise my eyes so I can see Lathan's reaction in the mirror. His gorgeous face is tight, and his biceps are flexing beautifully from his strong grip on the tub rim.

"More?" I ask while gripping his hips and holding still since I can't tell if he's experiencing pain or pleasure.

"Yes," he croaks out, so I thrust forward until Lathan cries out and then bites down on his forearm.

"You okay?" I ask, needing him to say he is so I that can move before I explode.

"Uh-huh," he mutters.

"If it's too much, tell me," I remind him before I pull almost all the way out and then plunge back into his tight warmth that's so good I could die a happy man right this second.

"*Ahh,*" he groans, but he doesn't tell me to stop, so I do it again and again, a little faster and harder each time.

"You feel so...goddamn...good," I tell Lathan. Thanks to my earlier releases, I last longer than normal, enjoying each and every slide into his body, the blissful whimpers he makes, the way his shoulders finally relax and his eyes drift closed in pleasure.

"*Ahhh, God*! Fuck, Pax," Lathan moans, meeting and holding my eyes in the mirror, telling me he's okay. Not only that, but he can take more. He wants more. So I give it to him until we're both panting messes, slumped against the rim of the tub.

"That was..." Lathan starts, and I brace myself for the next word. "Intense."

"Yeah," I agree, unsure if that's a good thing or bad thing. "You doing okay?" I ask him while kissing away the moisture droplets on his back.

"I'm still in shock," he replies, not really answering the question.

"Lathan?" I ask. "Just give it to me straight."

"Well," he begins. "We should probably drain the water because I came all in it."

"You did?" I ask in surprise. "Without using your hand?" He held on to the tub the whole time, so I know he didn't jerk himself off.

"You're not making fun of me, are you?" he asks before he turns around to face me, slowly lowering himself down again with his back against the wall.

"No, definitely not," I tell him. "Does that mean you enjoyed yourself?"

"I would say so, yeah," he replies with a nod and half a grin. "At first I was too tense, and it was so...different. But then, yeah..."

"Yeah?" I repeat with a smile.

"Even so, you're not going near my ass again for a few days," he replies.

"I was a little sore after the other day. But based on earlier, it does get easier," I assure him.

"Good," he says. "So, now can we get a quick shower and then go to bed? I'm wiped out."

"Hell yes," I agree, leaning forward to kiss him briefly. "I missed you," I tell him again rather than say the three other words trying to escape from my lips. Ones I've never said to anyone other than Roxy and Nana and don't plan on saying so soon.

Against my lips, Lathan says, "I'm glad you're back. And I'm even happier that I have tomorrow off. No practice. No films. Just me and you."

"That is awesome," I tell him, glad to get some time together. "Would you like to go see the house that I just bought tomorrow?"

"You bought a house? For the club?" he asks with a big smile. "When?"

"A few days ago, before I left," I answer with a shrug. "Oh, and I've decided on a name."

"Let's hear it," he says.

"*Moby Dick's.*"

"*Moby Dick's.* That's...very gay but funny," he jokes with a chuckle. "I'm guessing you're gonna have a big whale on the sign?"

"Of course. What else would I use?" I ask. "A big dick?"

"Yep, the whale is better," he agrees. "Congrats, and I can't wait to see it –" Lathan starts before his sentence trails off and his face falls.

"You can't be seen there," I finish for him. And it sucks because this is the most exciting thing I've ever done in my life and I can't share it with Lathan, at least not firsthand.

"I'm sorry," he says, reaching up to stroke his palm over the side of my face tenderly. "But I want to help you get the house ready. It's gonna be great, Pax."

"Yeah, I think so too," I reply, even if I hate the fact that the most important man in my life won't even be there on opening day.

But I knew from day one that Lathan was in the closet and that fact wouldn't be changing anytime soon. I care about him, and I meant it when I told him I could wait for him.

I just wish I didn't have to.

CHAPTER 21

Lathan

I've just crashed on the sofa after practice when there's a knock on the door. Too tired to get up again I simply call out, "Come in!" since I know it's unlocked.

The door creaks open slowly, and then Kelsey says, "Hey!", when she comes around to the living room.

"Hey," I reply. Her hair is in an up-do off of her neck, and she's clutching a notebook, making her look like a sexy school girl. "I'm flat out beat," I tell her.

"Rough practice?" she asks, taking a seat next to me, so close I can smell her sweet, floral scent.

"Brutal," I reply.

"Still want to do this tonight?" she asks hesitantly.

"Yeah, of course. Ask away," I assure her since I know she's been working hard on wedding arrangements the last few days based on her text messages.

"I checked your schedule, and there's a home game next weekend, so...

"Next weekend?" I repeat in surprise because it sounds so soon. Too soon. I could be getting married in just days, and I still haven't told Pax. I've tried, but every time I chicken out, too afraid of losing him.

"Yeah, you said the sooner, the better, right?" Kelsey asks timidly, holding the book in front of her chest like a shield.

"Right. Yes. I said that. Next week works."

"Great," she replies, blowing out a breath. "The church you told me about, First Baptist, is free Saturday too. If that place is still okay, I'll confirm tomorrow."

"Sure," I agree since that's the same church where my parents were married thirty-four years ago. Do I feel guilty about saying vows I don't mean in a church where I was taught not to lie? A little, but it's for the greater good --- my mom's life that's currently hanging by an unraveling thread.

"Does eleven o'clock work for the ceremony? I know you have a game Sunday night, so I didn't want it to be too late by the time we have the reception and all."

"Eleven is good. We can stay at my parents' house the night before if you want," I offer so that we can be close to the church.

"That would be great. I'll have someone do my hair and makeup at the church early that morning. And I'm going dress shopping tomorrow," Kelsey says as she opens the notebook and her eyes move down one of the pages. "Oh, if you don't have one, you'll need to get fitted for a tux."

"Right, a tux."

"Can you do that tomorrow after practice? I could text you the addresses of a few places for you to pick from which is most convenient."

Wow. Kelsey is amazing. She's thought of everything and is trying her best to make this as easy for me with my busy schedule as possible when she's the one doing me the favor.

"Okay, yeah," I agree even though I would rather be seeing Pax after practice.

"How do you feel about Wildcats colors?"

"They're fine, why?" I ask in confusion.

"No, I meant for the wedding colors," she replies with a smile.

"Oh, right, of course," I say in understanding. "Blue and yellow works."

"And I guess you don't care much about the flowers, food, or decorations?" she asks while flipping to another page in her notebook.

"Nope. Whatever you think is best," I tell her.

"Great, so if you'll get your tux and give me your list of guests with addresses, that should be it for your part," she says. "But I sort of need the list ASAP so I can get the invitations printed and mailed tomorrow since it's such short notice for the guests."

"I'll work on it tonight and email you tomorrow morning at the latest," I assure her.

"And just to make sure, you do still want to go through with this, right?" she asks. "I mean, once the invitations go out, it would be really embarrassing if we didn't..."

"I want to do this," I tell her, placing my palm on her knee to stop it from bouncing with nervousness. "The question is, do you want to?"

"I do," she answers followed by a smile. "I think what your mom is going through is awful, and this is so sweet of you to do for her," she says, covering my hand with hers and giving it a squeeze. "But if you leave me at the altar, Lathan Savage, I'll very likely die of humiliation and come back to haunt you."

"That won't happen," I tell her since this is what I know my mom needs. My only concern is how the hell I'm supposed to tell Pax...

"What about the media?" she asks. "I wasn't sure how low-key you wanted this to be?"

"No media," I say without hesitation. "We can tell them afterward, but I don't want to have to deal with all the questions and cameras, not until it's all over. That would be stressful and not good for my mom to have to deal with them all in her face, so can we just keep it quiet?"

"Sure," Kelsey replies. "I'm only inviting a few family members and close friends who don't even watch football, so you won't have to worry about them squealing."

"Good. That's good. Let's just keep it small and intimate."

"Agreed," she says, lowering her eyes to her hands now in her lap. "So, what's the plan for me moving in with you?"

"Ah, I guess we can do that the week after the wedding. Everything is gonna be pretty hectic before, right? Do you need more money for movers?"

"No, that's okay. I think I can haul everything over in a few trips."

"No way," I tell her with a shake of my head. "I'll help, and we can recruit Quinton and Kohen too, if needed. Maybe after we watch game films that Monday?"

"Okay, that will work," she agrees. "So, I guess that's everything. I'll make the plans for the rehearsal and dinner the night before, then let you know when to be where."

"Thanks again for doing all this, Kelsey. I definitely owe you," I tell her since she's making a legally binding commitment of marriage with me, knowing it will eventually end in divorce when...

No, my mom is gonna get her treatments, and this time they *will* work. If Kelsey and I have to stay married or have a pretend breakup if she decides to date someone else, we'll figure it out down the road. Way down the road hopefully.

And Pax, well, I'll tell him after the wedding, because I'm scared that if I mention it to him before he'll try to talk me out of it. This is not about me or him. This is about my mom and giving her a chance to see her only son walk down the aisle even if the cancer continues to spread.

"I'm glad I could be the one to help you," Kelsey says before she leans over and kisses my cheek, then gets to her feet. "Don't forget to send me your list tonight!" she reminds me as she lets herself out.

While I'm thinking about it, I pull up my phone and start going through my contacts, deciding who to invite to my last-minute wedding. I copy and paste names and addresses into a message later that night and send it to Kelsey, also asking if she would like to go see my parents this weekend. Her affirmative response is almost instantaneous.

Now that that's taken care of, I find the willpower to get up and head to bed. There, I switch over to the chat log I have with Pax, so far only a few short messages. Undoing my jeans, I shove them and my boxer briefs down far enough to pull my cock out and start stroking it until it's nice and hard. Then, I take a photo and send it to him with the message, "Wish you were here." While lying in bed, waiting for his response, I drift off to sleep.

...

Pax

"W*ish you were here."*

Those words wouldn't normally constitute a booty call request. But throw in the photo of Lathan's Moby Dick and, well, he's just begging for me to come over and fuck around with him.

And I'm more than happy to oblige.

Not bothering to change out of my gray sweats, I slip on a white tee and my shoes, the most casually dressed I've ever left the house, then head out to my BMW with my phone in one hand and my keys in the other. For this short trip at night, I don't even bother with my wallet.

I should be ashamed that I'm such an eager slut for the tight end or feel insulted that he expects me to drop what I'm doing to come get him off on a Wednesday night. But, nah, it's so worth it.

When I arrive at Lathan's place, I walk up the sidewalk and knock on the door. Then I wait and wait and wait some more for him to answer it. He must have hopped in the shower after he sent me that message.

I try the doorknob, and it turns easily, so I push it open and step inside the silent apartment, turning the deadbolt to lock it behind me. Lathan is crazy to leave his door unlocked at night even for a few minutes. He's hot, rich, and famous with practically a painted, red bullseye on his front door inviting stalkers or robbers inside.

"Lathan?" I call out when he doesn't appear. Walking further into the apartment that's completely dark, I stumble around until I find the bedroom where...my boy is passed out cold.

Ohh-kay.

So either he fell asleep waiting for me, or I was wrong, and his message wasn't an implied booty call.

Now I feel stupid. But I haven't seen him in a few days, so I'm eager to spend time with him even if it's just the two of us sleeping in the same bed.

So, now I can either stay and look like a fool or go back home where I'll just be wishing I was here in bed with Lathan.

Sucking up my pride and hoping he won't throw me out, I get undressed and slip underneath the covers on the empty side of the mattress. Even in the darkness, I can tell Lathan's backside is dark, which means he's wearing his shirt and boxer briefs, so he obviously wasn't waiting for me to come and ravage him.

Still unable to make myself leave, I slide over behind him until we're spooning and wrap my arm around his waist.

"Pax?" he asks softly, his voice deep and gravelly.

"Yeah, it's me," I whisper to him.

"Good," he says on a sigh before his breathing grows louder and he falls back asleep.

I'm not far behind him.

…

"Pax? *Pax!*"

Lathan's voice wakes me out of a deep sleep. My limbs are still paralyzed, and there's drool on my pillow where I'm passed out, curled up on my side.

"Hmm?" I mutter.

"Pax, you need to leave," Lathan says. "It's almost nine."

"Mmm," I agree.

"Now, Pax! What if someone sees you leaving my house and realizes you stayed over?" he asks. "You shouldn't be here!"

The anger in his usually calm, mellow voice wakes me the fuck up quicker than a bucket of hot coffee.

I blink my eyes open and find a glowering Lathan looming over me, his blond hair wet from his shower and dressed in black athletic pants and a Wildcats tee.

"You didn't complain last night," I remind him as I try to get more awake.

"What do you mean? Did we..." he asks, eyes going wide.

"Yes, Lathan. I sneak into men's beds and fuck them while they're unconscious," I huff. "No, we didn't do anything but sleep. You were happy I was here, though."

"You know that you can't just show up like this and stay over! People could see you. My neighbors could see you!"

"Excuse the fuck out of me," I tell him grumpily as I sit up and throw my legs over the side of the bed. "But what the hell did you expect after that dick pic you sent me?" I ask him.

"I don't have time for this," Lathan says while rubbing his temples with his thumb and fingers. "Don't show up here again unless I send you a fucking invitation."

"Fuck you," I tell his back as he walks away, pissed that he's so mad about me being here. He doesn't have to be such a dick about it.

Looking for what's within my reach, I see the remote on the bedside table, pick it up, and throw it at him, hitting him right on his incredible ass. The remote falls and the batteries in the back of it scatter over the bedroom floor. That makes Lathan pause. But only for a moment.

Instead of retaliating like I'd hoped and having our fight end up with angry sex or even an angry kiss, Lathan just keeps walking. And then I hear the sound of the front door open and close.

What the hell is his problem?

Last night, when he was sleep-drunk, he acted like he was glad I was here, and then he starts yelling at me this morning?

I get that he doesn't want to be outed, but fuck. He doesn't have to get so bent out of shape. There's only a small chance that someone could see me here, but I guess I'm just not worth the risk.

CHAPTER 22

Lathan

"There's the crazy SOB, soon-to-be-married man!" Quinton says when I walk into the locker room before practice. "Are you seriously tying the knot with my nanny?" he asks me with a slap to my upper arm.

"I seriously am," I reply, shoving down my anger at Pax for being so reckless. While I put on my pads, I try to tell myself I shouldn't feel guilty for jumping down his throat this morning. He should've known better than to stay overnight with me. More than ever, I can't have any rumors flying around right now.

When I woke up with Pax in my bed, the first thing I felt was contentment. That quickly shifted to concern that someone could've seen him come into my townhouse or would see him leaving. If that happens and someone turns a photo into the media, I'm fucked. The wedding would be off, and my parents would know I lied to them. Everything would be ruined.

Pax and I have to be more careful, and he doesn't seem to understand that. If Kelsey had seen him at my place, she might have told Callie, who would tell Quinton! Then my secret would be out.

Remembering that my best friend should be angry at me, I go over to Quinton to talk to him. Lowering my voice, I tell him. "Sorry about giving Kelsey that ring. I'm gonna buy another one tonight when I go out to get my tux and switch them up. She'll never know the difference."

When I ask Kelsey to trade rings, I'm sure she'll be on board. That girl would go along with anything I ask, fortunately.

"No problem," Quinton says with his crooked grin. "Callie loved it, so at least I know I didn't fuck up by picking that one out."

"That's true," I agree, exhaling in relief that he's not gonna rip my head off.

"So, when's the big day?" he asks, sitting down on the bench in front of his locker.

"Next Saturday."

"Next Saturday!" Quinton shouts in surprise.

"Yep, Saturday, December third. Eleven o'clock. Your invitation is in the mail," I tell him.

"Wow. You're not wasting any time, are you?" he asks. "Are you sure you two are not rushing things?"

"No, Kelsey and I both agree that sooner is better," I answer him honestly.

"I still can't believe it," he says with a shake of his head. "Who would've guessed the virgin would get hitched before me?"

My face burns bright at the reminder that, as far as women go, I guess you could say I'm still a virgin.

"Wait a second," Quinton starts. "You're not, like, saving yourself for marriage, are you? Is that the reason for the hurry?"

"Maybe," I reply since that makes more sense than admitting we're rushing to get married before my mom dies.

No, fuck that. She's not gonna die. Mom has sounded so excited and strong on the phone the last few times I've talked to her. And dad said she's not sleeping as often during the day.

This Friday, when I take Kelsey home to meet them, I plan to try and talk to her about resuming the treatments.

During practice, I still can't shake the argument I had with Pax this morning, and it completely throws me off my game. I can't catch worth a shit, and I know I won't be able to shake this shit until I apologize to him. The problem is, with everything going on, I don't know when I'll even get to see him again.

...

"Mom, Dad, I want you to meet Kelsey," I tell my parents when my soon-to-be-wife and I are standing in their living room Friday afternoon.

"Such a beautiful girl!" my mom says before she throws her frail arms around Kelsey. "I'm so glad to finally meet you!"

"Welcome to the family," my dad says with a broad smile before he takes a turn hugging Kelsey, too.

"Come in and have a seat," my mom tells us before shuffling over to sit down in her rocking chair. Unlike the last few times I've seen her, she's dressed in stretch pants and a baggy tee instead of a nightgown, and she's wearing one of her blonde wigs that is cut in a short bob like how her hair was before the most recent round of chemo started a few weeks ago.

"I want to know everything! How you met, how long you've been dating. Spill it all," she says.

Still clasping Kelsey's hand, I pull her over to the loveseat so we can sit next to each other. Hopefully, we can find our way through the third degree from my parents so that it ends with them believing we're in love.

"Well, I'm not sure if Lathan told you or not, but I'm Quinton's nanny," Kelsey starts, not the least bit reserved in her response. "That's where we met a few weeks ago, at Quinton and Callie's.

Lathan was too shy to ask me out, so I got up my nerve and just said to him, 'Hey, would you like to have dinner with me sometime?'"

"And of course, he said yes," my mom chimes in with a smile.

"He tried to give me excuses about being busy with practice and games, but I wouldn't take no for an answer," Kelsey adds while patting my forearm with her free hand.

"That sounds like Lathan," my dad says with a grin in response to the made-up story.

"Best decision I've ever made," I say honestly while looking at Kelsey, knowing she understands my meaning.

"So when's the big day?" my mom asks.

"You should get your invitation later today or tomorrow," Kelsey tells my parents practically bursting with excitement. "We're getting married next Saturday!"

"*Next Saturday*?" my dad repeats. "Like a week from tomorrow?"

"Yeah," I answer. "December third. Do either of you have plans?" I tease them.

"Where?" my mom asks with less enthusiasm because she's likely worried about whether or not she will feel up to traveling. "In Wilmington?"

"No, here, at First Baptist Church," Kelsey answers. "I've already made the arrangements with Preacher Roberts."

My mom slaps her palm over her gaping mouth while tears begin to swim in her silver eyes. "Thank you," she says, her voice breaking with emotion. "I'm so glad it's going to be close...and in *our* church..."

"Wow, I don't know what to say," my father adds, also sounding choked up. "This is just wonderful. We're so happy for you two."

"Oh, I'm a mess! Please excuse me for a moment," my mom says before she tries to rise from her seat and fails. Dad jumps up before I can to help her to her feet, and then she shuffles down the hall and into the bathroom.

"She okay?" I ask him.

"Yeah, I think she's just happy and a little overwhelmed," he replies.

"Do you think this is all too much for her? Should we postpone?" I ask in concern. Maybe this wasn't a good idea after all to spring everything on my mom so soon.

"No, no, it's fine. She's happy for you. We both are," he tells me with a wave of his hand. "But still, I have to ask, are you two sure this is what you want? I understand the rush; and while I'm grateful on your mother's behalf that you want her to be a part of this, I just don't want you to think you have to..."

"It's my fault," Kelsey jumps in and says. "I didn't want to wait, and Lathan was sweet enough that he agreed."

Nodding, my dad is silent in thought a moment before he asks, "You're not...pregnant, are you?"

"What? No!" I exclaim. "Definitely not."

"Good," my father says on a sigh of relief. "I didn't want this to be a shotgun wedding that eventually ended badly either."

"Nope, no babies, Dad," I assure him.

"Not yet at least," Kelsey adds with a smile. "But that could change soon, right?" she looks up and asks me, brown eyes so sincere about us not only fucking but reproducing that they cause a knot of worry in my gut. Or maybe that's my upchuck reflex.

Before I can comment, though, she kisses me on the lips, silencing me before I can say anything to ruin our believability. At the touch of her tongue on mine in front of my father, I quickly pull away and apologize to him.

"Don't mind me," he says, getting up from his seat. "I'll just go check on your mother."

"What was *that*?" I whisper to Kelsey as soon as he's out of sight.

Speaking quickly under her breath, she says, "You looked like you were gonna puke from the thought of kids, so I tried to get your mind off of it. Besides, don't you want your mom to look forward to the future, not just you married but giving her grandchildren too?"

"Ah, yeah," I agree. "But can we not make out in front of my parents in their living room?"

"Lathan, we're getting married. That's what couples who plan to spend the rest of their life together do. We're trying to sell it and make it look real, aren't we?"

"Yes, but..."

"Then you have to get used to kissing me without flinching away like you're gonna be sick."

"I don't flinch away!" I argue.

"Yeah, you do," Kelsey replies sadly. "Is there something wrong with me?" Cupping her palm to her mouth, she asks, "Oh God. Do I need a Tic Tac?"

"No, no, of course not," I assure her. "I'm just...not very experienced." I use that truth as my excuse. Kelsey is only one of the two women I've ever kissed.

"I know you're not," she says. "That's why we need to practice, to help you loosen up and make it more natural."

"Right, you're right," I agree. "Let's um...kiss me," I tell her, bracing myself and telling my body not to cringe away.

"You sure?" she asks with an arched eyebrow.

"Yes," I say, but instead of waiting for her to make a move, I take the lead. Turning toward her and leaning down, I slant my mouth over hers. Hell, I even slip her my tongue that she greedily accepts before she reaches up and holds my face to give me a taste of hers.

It's not a bad kiss, by any means. Kelsey is actually a really good kisser. Not as good as Pax, but I doubt many people are that amazing since he's had plenty of practice. In fact, our kiss goes on for so long, my dick gets hard, making me mutter a relieved curse that I'm not gay. There's some small comfort in knowing that I can actually get it up for a woman.

Do I want to have sex with Kelsey?

Fuck no.

That's not even something I have to consider. I want Pax. Only Pax. And there are not enough female kisses in the world to change my mind.

Now I just have to apologize for yelling at him the other morning and hope he'll forgive me. Oh, and pray that he doesn't find out I'm getting married before it's done.

First, I need to take care of business here.

Pulling away from Kelsey, I ask her, "Was that better?"

"Oh yeah," she mutters, eyes still half closed.

"Good. We'll convince everyone after we say our vows," I assure her. "For now, let me go check on my mom and I'll be right back," I say as I get to my feet.

"Sure, of course. Go," Kelsey urges.

Down the hallway, I find my parents in their bedroom sitting on the side of the bed, with my mom crying on my father's chest.

"Mom! What's the matter? Why are you upset?" I ask frantically as I go over and kneel down in front of her.

"I'm so...so stubborn," she says through the tears, reaching a trembling hand out to cup my face. "I almost missed this...because I was ready to surrender."

"No, you can't give up," I tell her as dampness coats my cheeks.

"I know. I won't," she agrees.

"Does that mean you'll keep doing the treatments?" I ask, holding my breath for her answer.

Mom nods before she replies. "Yes. Yes, whatever it takes to stay here with you both," she says, squeezing my father tighter and pulling me to her.

"Thank you," I tell her, pressing my cheek to her chest. Hearing her fragile heart beating and feeling her warmth, I know that this time the chemo and radiation are going to work.

They have to.

...

Pax

"What are you doing here?" I ask Lathan when I open my front door and find him standing on the sidewalk. His hands are shoved into his navy-blue hoodie pockets and there's an earnest look on his gorgeous face. "I didn't send you an invitation, did I?" I ask snottily, throwing his words back at him even if I've missed the asshole like crazy these last few days.

"I'm sorry," he says softly. "I've got a lot of shit going on, and I've been stressed out. I wanted you there. That was never the issue."

"You think I would do something to intentionally out you?" I ask, leaning my shoulder against the open door and crossing my arms over my chest.

"No, of course not. I'm just paranoid and worried it could happen, ending my career. My parents depend on my salary and all, so..."

"Oh. I didn't know that," I reply, feeling bad when I realize he's never really talked about his family to me and I've never asked.

"Yeah, so I'm sorry I snapped at you when it's my issues, ones that don't have anything to do with you," Lathan says. "Will you forgive me?"

"Hmm," I mutter in mock thought. "It's gonna cost you..."

"Anything," he replies, licking his lips like he either expects me to make him get on his knees or because he *wants* to get on his knees.

"Fine," I agree. "I'll let you decide on your retribution."

"Then let me in to get started," he says with a relieved grin, making him even more boyishly handsome.

"Sure," I say opening the door wider. "I think it's finally time for that sixty-nine position I told you about."

"Fuck, yes," Lathan says when he comes in. While I'm locking up for the night, he says, "I love your mouth and I love your cock, so I can't wait to have both at the same time."

Did he just use the word *love*?

While he was only talking about my body parts, I can't help but hope he's starting to fall for the rest of me too.

CHAPTER 23

Lathan

Between brutal practices, wedding planning and the bachelor party Quinton and the guys insisted on dragging me to last night, I haven't been able to make time to see Pax all week or, hell, even text him. From the moment I wake up until I fall into bed at night, someone is telling me to do something.

There's also the nagging guilt in my gut that's had me avoiding Pax in the few moments I get free from life and football. I fucking hate keeping this from him. It's killing me to withhold something so important, but growing up it was always easier to ask for forgiveness than get permission from my parents whenever I wanted to do something I knew they wouldn't approve of. This is the same situation.

I'm just not sure Pax will understand how important it is that I give my mother this wedding. He'll be pissed. And if he causes a scene, the wedding might get put off.

Once it's done, I can tell Pax everything that's going on with her illness, and he can even meet Kelsey since I plan on telling her the truth too. Eventually. If Pax and I are going to see each other with her as a front, then she deserves to know what I'm hiding. All of it. Then I'll have to pray she doesn't tell Callie, Quinton or anyone else.

God, it feels like I'm being pulled in a million different directions, trying to make my mom happy, worrying about how bad the cancer is, not wanting to let my dad down, or my team, not doing anything to ruin this perfect wedding Kelsey has been planning, and then finally, not hurting Pax and hoping he cares about me enough to understand why I'm doing this.

Pax is not close with his parents, but I would like to think that he loves his grandmother enough to do something like this for her if she were sick. Does he love me enough to forgive me?

After Kelsey and I are married, I can show Pax that *nothing* between he and I will change just because we're husband and wife. When it's done, I'll be able to prove to him that I don't want Kelsey or have feelings for her, especially after I tell her that Pax and I are together. That, if nothing else, will prove to him how much I care for him since he knows I haven't ever told anyone about the two of us for fear of the repercussions.

This afternoon, Kelsey and I are driving up to Elon for our rehearsal and to have dinner with both sides of our family. My mom is even feeling good enough to come out. Soon Pax will know everything, but for now, I send him a text telling him a partial truth --- I'm going to see my parents for the weekend and I'll come over to his place when I get back either late tomorrow night or early Sunday morning.

Just one more day of keeping all of this from him, and he'll either say he understands or tell me we're through.

I don't know what the fuck I'll do if he says we're over.

...

Pax

. . .

What the fuck is going on with Lathan?

I've barely seen or heard from him this past week after he apologized and we made up from our fight. He's only been over once whereas before he was coming over almost every night.

Several times I've texted him with no response, but I refuse to send any more and look like a desperate asshole. Even if I am a desperate asshole.

Could he have met someone else?

No way.

Lathan is still so shy with me, even after he's been balls deep inside me on more than one occasion. And he still hasn't stopped blushing when he gives me a blowjob.

So, why is he ignoring me?

Tonight's Friday, and he did text me earlier to say he was going to stay with his parents this weekend but that he would try to come over late tomorrow night. However, that still doesn't explain his absence the other six days this week after he promised he wouldn't ignore me like before.

I could stop by his place, but that just seems too...stalkerish and a bad idea. Paxton Price doesn't stalk like some crazy ex-girlfriend. Especially not after Lathan freaked the fuck out the last time I came over uninvited.

When my phone rings, I lurch across the sofa to grab it from the end table to answer, hoping it's him. Seeing Roxy's name on the caller ID is only slightly disappointing. Maybe she's seen Lathan. Although, it's not like I can come right out and ask her about him without it sounding suspicious. I love my best friend and would trust her with my life, but not with Lathan's secret.

"Hey, Rox, what's up? How's practice and shit been going?" I ask in a rush because I'm just not in the mood to talk.

"Ah, good. Great, thanks. How have you been?" she asks.

"Fine. Perfect. Awesome," I say. "Getting the club ready is keeping me busy."

Thank fuck. Without all the planning this week on finalizing renovations in the house, buying furniture, and hiring staff, I would've been out of my mind.

"Oh, I bet," Roxy replies. "But do you think you can spare an afternoon of dress shopping with me today?"

"Dress shopping?" I repeat, not too excited by the idea since I'm in my sweats. "Why are you asking *me* to go shopping with you? Because I'm gay you think I'm supposed to be the best shopping companion?" I tease.

"Noooo," she drawls. "I'm asking you to go with me because you're my only friend and Kohen would have me in a clubbing dress if I asked his opinion."

"That is true," I agree with a smile. "Fine. Let's shop. What's the occasion?"

"A wedding, tomorrow."

"Why in the hell did you wait until the day before to go find a dress?" I ask her in confusion.

"It came up suddenly," she says. "Meet me at the mall and we can catch up while we shop, 'kay?" she asks.

"Yeah, yeah," I mutter. "Let me put some clothes on, and I'll be there. Wanna grab dinner at the Italian place in the food court first?" I offer.

"Heck yeah," she says. "Love ya!"

"Love you, Rox," I reply before ending the call and hauling myself up to get ready.

At least shopping will keep me busy this afternoon rather than dwell on what the hell is going on with my boyfriend. Not that Lathan is technically my boyfriend, but that's the direction I thought we were heading in before he up and disappeared on me this week.

...

"He's getting a quick shower before the rehearsal. Can I take a message for him?" she asks sweetly.

"No. No, that's okay," I tell her before ending the call.

And then I sit there staring at my phone, unable to move. How could he do this to me? I trusted him! I truly believed that he actually cared about me, and he's marrying someone tomorrow?

I can't fucking believe it.

My heart is crumbling because I never expected Lathan to hurt me like this. All this time, he was just using me for sex, fulfilling his curiosity. Experimenting. He obviously didn't give a shit about me. If he did, he wouldn't be marrying someone else!

I'm still sitting in my car in the cold night air when Roxy comes up and knocks on the door's window.

When I open the door to talk to her, she says, "Pax? What are you doing still sitting here? It's freezing! At least crank the car."

"I'm so fucking stupid," I tell Roxy.

"What? Pax, you're not stupid. Don't say that," she says, kneeling down next to the seat with her hand squeezing my arm.

"I thought coming out was the hardest thing I would ever have to do, but it's not," I mutter. "It's dealing with the assholes who are too scared to do it themselves. And knowing there's nothing I can do about it."

"Aww, I'm sorry," Roxy says, reaching up to wipe away the single teardrop that came to a rest on my cheek. "You'll find someone, Pax. I know you will. You've just had back luck."

Bad luck? Yeah, the bad luck of being a gay man who only falls for closet cases.

"Sorry to bail on you, Rox, but I need to go home," I tell her, finally finding the wherewithal to crank the car and drive again.

"Yeah, no, it's fine," she says when she stands up and leans down to kiss my cheek. "Love you. Call me later, 'kay?"

"Okay," I reply before I finally pull away, heading back to my lonely apartment.

CHAPTER 24

Lathan

"I now pronounce you husband and wife. You may kiss your bride."

Those words sound so strange coming from my childhood preacher while I stand at the altar next to Kelsey, our friends and family watching on.

I thought saying "I do" would be harder than it was, knowing it was a lie, but that was the easy part. Even reaching for Kelsey's face to pull it to mine and kiss her is a piece of cake now that I've had some practice.

The hardest part is thinking about what Pax will say tomorrow after it's done and over when there's no going back.

"Everything looks perfect for tomorrow," my mom says from the first pew.

"It does," Kelsey's mom agrees when she goes over to sit next to

Mom. "And don't they just make such a lovely couple? Our grand-kids are going to be adorable!"

I plaster on a fake smile and take Kelsey's hand to lead her over to where our parents are talking.

"I don't know about you all, but I'm starving," I say, ready to get out of the church now that the quick rehearsal is done.

"Ditto," Quinton agrees. He's here with Callie and Brady tonight because he's agreed to be my best man. They're all staying at a nearby hotel so they can get to the church early tomorrow.

"We'll meet you at the steakhouse?" I ask. There are not a ton of places to eat around here, but Kelsey thankfully thought to call ahead and find a place to seat all sixteen of us tonight.

"Lathan," my mom says softly when Dad helps her to her feet.

"Yeah, Mom? Are you okay?" I ask her, taking hold of her elbow when she sways.

"I think your father and I are going to head on home, if that's okay with you and Kelsey? I need to save up my energy for the big day tomorrow."

"Sure," I tell her, hating that she doesn't have the energy to go with us all to dinner.

"We'll see you and Kelsey back at the house later, right?" Dad asks.

"Right. We shouldn't be too late," I assure him.

"Take your time," he urges. "I know you have a ton of things to do."

"I think Kelsey has it all under control," I tell him, glancing down at her while giving her hand a squeeze.

"You're lucky to have found her," my mom says with a smile, leaning up to kiss my cheek and then hug Kelsey.

"Yeah, I am," I agree, because I am thankful I found someone so understanding of my situation and trustworthy enough to keep our arrangement a secret.

"No, I'm the lucky one," Kelsey says, giving my arm a squeeze.

"Your son is the sweetest, most caring man I've ever met. I know you're proud of him."

"We are," my dad says, hugging us both before he and my mom leave and we grab our coats to follow them out.

Once we're in my Jeep with the heat going, Kelsey fastens her seatbelt in the passenger seat and says, "Did your mom decide to start treatments again?"

"She did," I look over and tell her with a smile. "And all thanks to you," I add sincerely. "You're freaking amazing for letting me talk you into legally becoming my wife. No matter what happens with my mom...well, it'll be some small comfort to remember her being here with me on my wedding day. That's priceless, you know?"

"I know," she replies with a smile. "If it were my mom, I would hope a wonderful man like yourself would do the same for me."

"Anything you ever want or need, just ask. I'm not sure if I'll ever be able to repay you," I tell her.

"Let's just start with you not getting cold feet tomorrow," she says, followed by a laugh.

"No cold feet," I promise. "I was ready to make it official tonight."

And that's the truth.

I'm ready to have this whole wedding deal done so I can see Pax, tell him what I've done and why, and pray he doesn't end the best thing I've ever had in my life.

CHAPTER 25

Pax

Saturday morning, after drinking myself to sleep, I wake up to the sound of my phone pinging with a text message. Reaching for it blindly on the nightstand, I grab it and pull it to me, figuring it's Roxy.

I have to blink my painfully swollen eyes several times to make sure they aren't playing tricks on me.

In my hand is a photo from Lathan, one of him with his cock in his hand telling me he woke up thinking about me this morning, how much he's missed me this week, and that he wants to see me tonight.

Tonight.

The night he's getting married!

Is he fucking kidding me?

I am so sick of this bullshit!

I have never outed anyone, but this so-called fiancée of Lathan's deserves to know the truth before she marries him. He'll never be satisfied with just her if he was fucking me while with her too.

Having her stand him up at the altar, making a fool out of him, would almost make up for this unrelenting pain in my chest threatening to split it wide open.

Decision made, I decide to get up and take a shower. I'm going to be making a trip to Elon today.

...

From my parking spot near the marina's entrance, I watch for Kohen or Roxy's car. And when I see them pull out, I follow them, staying close enough to keep up but not too close for them to see me. Thankfully, my black BMW blends in well with traffic rather than sticks out.

Before I out him to his fiancée, I want to talk to Lathan face-to-face, to give him a chance to call off this sham of a wedding before he goes through with it. Even if he doesn't care about me, he liked what we did together. Otherwise, he wouldn't have cheated on his fiancée not once but many, many times.

All these weeks I thought he was just shy and inexperienced, but it turns out he must have been hesitant because of his guilt.

Pulling into the church that's several hours away from Wilmington, I park and wait for Roxy and Kohen to go inside before I climb out of my car and follow them. Luckily, they got here early, so there are not many guests wandering around yet.

I open the front door of the small church, hoping to creep quietly through to find Lathan without running into anyone, especially someone I know who would question why I'm here. I make it about five steps through the door when a thin, frail lady with a perfectly cut blonde bob steps out of the women's restroom and sees me.

"Hi, are you here for the bride or groom?" she asks with a broad smile on her face.

Wavering on what I should say, I decide to go with the truth.

"Ah, the groom. Actually, I *really* need to talk to him. Do you know where can I find him?"

"Lathan's right through here," she says, slowly leading me down a narrow hallway. Stopping outside the first closed door, she raises her knuckles to knock on it.

"Come in," Lathan's voice says from the other side, causing my heart to lurch.

"Go on in," she says, urging me forward, so I open the door and slip inside.

And there he is, even if my eyes can't believe what I'm seeing.

Lathan is standing in front of a floor length mirror wearing a navy-blue suit and straightening his yellow tie. That's when it really hits me that he's actually doing this. He's really here, in a church, getting ready to marry someone.

"Pax?" he exclaims in surprise when he finally notices me in the mirror's reflection. "What are you doing here?" Spinning around to face me, Lathan steps forward with his arms raised as if to hug me. When he's close enough to touch, I push his chest away, causing his forehead to crease.

"What are you...how did you..." Lathan stammers.

"What the fuck are you doing?" I ask him through clenched teeth.

Visibly deflating, his shoulders sag and he exhales heavily. "Pax, I swear I was gonna explain everything to you tonight..."

"Explain what exactly?" I shout. "That you're hiding who you really are? That you've been cheating on your fiancée this whole fucking time?"

"No. This wedding isn't about me..." he starts.

"What a load of shit!" I exclaim, poking him with a finger in his chest. "You're just like the rest, and I'm not sticking around to be some piece of side ass when your wife can't give you what you need!"

"Pax, it's not what you think. I can't explain it right now because I have to go. They're waiting for me to do pictures," he says.

"You can go somewhere all right," I tell him. "But if you walk out that door and do this, we're through!"

"Yeah," Lathan says sadly, lowering his eyes. His chin trembles and his jaw remains tightly clenched like my own. "That's probably for the best anyway. I'm sorry it had to be this way, that you found out before I could explain."

I'm still in a state of shock when he walks past me to leave the room.

"Fuck you," I call out to his back as he walks out and I'm left standing there in utter disbelief.

I can't believe this is fucking happening.

How could everything go from being so perfect with Lathan to this...over and done in a matter of days?

Why didn't I realize what was really going on?

I've never been enough for a man before, so it was stupid to think that was the case now.

Even as angry and hurt as I am, I can't bring myself to walk out the door and tell everyone the truth. Lathan's fiancée deserves to know, but it's not my place to tell her.

It's his.

"I'm sorry," the woman from earlier says, startling me because I didn't notice she had quietly stepped into the room.

"What for?" I ask, looking away to wipe away the moisture from underneath my eyes.

"Now I think I know why Lathan's doing this," she says. When she doesn't say anything else, I look over just as she reaches up and pulls off what I now realize is a wig, revealing her sparse, thinning blonde hair underneath.

Oh no. This woman's not just sickly; she has cancer.

"I'm Lathan's mother," she informs me, which is almost as shocking as finding out he was getting married.

"You..." I start, my eyes widening in horror, imagining how god awful her condition must be for him to deal with. That painful truth is only compounded by the fact that Lathan never once mentioned her to me.

"I have stage four pancreatic cancer," she tells me.

"Oh, my God," I mutter. More than being really sick; she's likely dying. "He never mentioned..."

"We've told Lathan he doesn't need to rush into this marriage, but I know he's doing it for me," she says with a small, tearful smile. "If he doesn't do it now, well, I would probably never get to see my son's wedding, so I've gone along with it. It's very selfish of me, I know. I'll try again to talk him out of it –"

"I'm sorry," I tell her.

"All I ever wanted for Lathan was for him to find *someone* to love him, so don't give up on him yet. Just give him a little more time."

"I just...I don't...why didn't he tell me the truth?" I stammer.

"Maybe because he's not ready to tell himself the truth," she replies, resting her palm gently on my back. "I need to go find my son and convince him that he doesn't have to do this today, but I'm really glad I got to meet you."

By the time she's left the room, all of my anger has deflated. How can I be mad at Lathan when he's doing this because his mom is dying?

And do I think she'll be able to change his mind?

No. Hell no.

Because I know Lathan. He's such an amazing, caring man with a huge heart. There's nothing that would stop him from giving this gift to his sick mother.

CHAPTER 26

Lathan

I'm married.

I have a wife.

I'm a husband.

This isn't how I imagined my wedding day would be, or who it would be with, but now it's done. Kelsey has been a godsend for planning such a beautiful event and going through with becoming my wife.

Even though my mom nearly convinced me to call off the wedding before the ceremony, there was just no way I could embarrass Kelsey like that and leave her at the altar. Besides, I wasn't ready to tell my mother I loved a man. Thankfully, she accepted my decision. In fact, I've never seen her so happy. And knowing that she's gonna start chemotherapy again next week has filled me with hope.

At the same time, I'm devastated that Pax showed up before I could explain everything to him. I'm not sure how he found out, maybe from Roxy, but what I do know is that he said he doesn't want to see me again.

That sure as fuck isn't what I wanted, but how can I expect him to keep sneaking around with me now that I'm married. It's not right for me to ask that of him, especially when I can't fathom ever coming out while I have a football contract. It wouldn't be fair to ask him to keep waiting or risk the chance of getting caught together, so I should just let him go no matter how much that hurts.

"This room is amazing," Kelsey says when the two of us finally step into our honeymoon suite at the hotel near the church after the long, crazy day.

"Yeah, the bed looks comfy," I agree, my body and soul so exhausted the floor is starting to look appealing to curl up on.

"It does," she agrees.

I don't know about her, but I'm ready to pass out. The last few days have been a whirlwind of practice and wedding planning.

"Would you mind unbuttoning me?" Kelsey asks, turning her back toward me and holding her long brown spirals off her neck to give me access.

"Sure," I say, starting with the button at the top of her satin gown and making my way down. "I'm not sure if I told you, but you looked gorgeous today."

"Thank you," she says over her shoulder as I keep going down the row of buttons. "It was a beautiful wedding. And your parents seemed happy."

"Yeah, my mom looked great," I agree. "Once she starts treatment next week, hopefully, we'll see some improvements on her next scan."

"I hope so," Kelsey agrees.

"There, last one," I tell her, my fingers flicking open the button at her lower back. My hands didn't even shake with nervousness like they would with most women. I guess that means that I'm getting comfortable around Kelsey now. And that's probably a good thing since she's now officially my wife.

When Kelsey turns back around to face me, she lets go of the hold she had on the front of her dress, and the whole thing falls into a puddle around her feet. She's not naked underneath it either. No, she's wearing a sexy, white lacy corset with sky-blue trim that pushes up her full breasts, a pair of tiny matching panties, and a garter belt that's clipped to the tops of her white thigh-high hose. The whole outfit ends with her white heels.

"Wow," I mutter involuntarily at the sight. And despite how hard I try, my eyes refuse to lift to her face like a gentleman. Then she turns around and starts for the bed, revealing her ass that looks amazing in the skimpy thong and garter straps.

"Are you, um, is that, ah, what you're sleeping in?" I ask, jerking on the knot of my tie that's getting tighter, right along with the crotch of my pants.

"Well," Kelsey says as she stretches out on her back in the center of the bed. "I was hoping you would take it off of me."

She wants me to help take her lingerie off. And I'm pretty sure it's just because of all the corset straps and...and...yeah.

"I don't know, Kelsey," I start, rubbing my palm over the back of my neck that's scalding hot. "This isn't...we shouldn't..."

"Don't be nervous," she says. "We're married now, so it's okay. This is what everyone does on their wedding night."

"Right, but this was all fake," I remind her with a wave of my hand, gesturing to the two of us.

"Come on, Lathan," Kelsey urges, going up on her knees on the mattress and looking even more tempting.

The devil on one of my shoulders reminds me that Pax said we were done, and that here's my chance to finally see how I like being with a woman. But the angel on the other side tells me that if I did that, I would only feel guilty afterward.

Fucking angel.

"Kelsey, I want to," I tell her. "I really do. But I'm sort of hung up on someone else..."

"Someone...someone else?" she asks with a confused crease

between her eyebrows when she sits back on her knees. "Then why didn't you just marry her?" Kelsey asks me, the hurt in her voice obvious without needing the help of her brown eyes misting over.

Goddammit. I don't mean to make her cry.

"It's not a she," I admit, deciding that she deserves for me to be honest with her after all she's sacrificed to marry me, even if Pax and I are over.

"What do you...*ohhh*," she mutters, eyes bulging in understanding. "You're...you're gay?"

"No! Yes. I don't know," I huff, throwing up my arms in the air. "I've never been with a woman, so..."

"Oh. I had no idea," Kelsey says. "Oh my God," she gasps, reaching down for the bed comforter to hold it up and cover the front of her body. "Now I feel so stupid."

"Don't," I tell her, taking a few steps to get closer to her. "You shouldn't. I'm an idiot for not telling you about this sooner."

"No, no, I'm stupid for thinking you would want to...after you made it clear this was just for your mom. Should I go?" she asks, glancing toward the door.

"No, stay," I tell her because I don't want to be alone tonight. If I am, that'll only remind me of Pax ending things and make me feel even shittier.

"So you have...a boyfriend?" Kelsey asks softly.

"Not anymore, if he was even that to begin with," I say. Trudging over to the bed, I sit on the edge to hang my head in my hands. "We sort of broke up earlier today," I admit to her. "He said we were through if I didn't call off the wedding."

"God, I'm sorry, Lathan," she says. Scooting over to me, Kelsey lifts her hand to my back and rubs it in comforting circles.

"It's my fault for keeping it from him," I explain. "Tonight, I was planning to tell him everything, how this would be good for us too, you know? That we could keep seeing each other without any rumors."

"You're gay," Kelsey repeats. "I still can't believe it. Who was the lucky guy?" she asks.

"Paxton Price."

She gasps and says, "Roxy's sexy and sharp dressed BFF?"

"Yep, that would be him."

"Oh, wow. He's hot. I've seen him at the games in the family box," she tells me. "Oh! And I bet he was the one who called your phone while you were in the shower last night."

"He called?" I look over my shoulder to ask her.

"Yeah, I forgot to tell you. His name didn't show up on the caller ID, and he didn't leave his name or a message. Guess I know why now." I never put Pax's name in my contact list, too afraid someone would see it.

"Roxy must have told him about the wedding," I guess.

"Must have," Kelsey agrees. Her hands move up to my shoulders, rubbing them, working the tension out of them. "Can we forget what I did earlier today and never speak of it again?" she asks. "I promise to never come on to you again."

"Deal," I easily agree, giving her a small smile. "Thanks for understanding and not hating me. And please don't tell anyone."

"Your secrets are all safe with me," she replies. "Now, let's get some sleep."

"I can sleep over on the pull-out sofa," I tell her.

"No, the bed's big enough for both of us," Kelsey points out, and it is soft and comfortable.

"Are you sure?" I ask.

"I'm sure you should sleep in the bed, and I'm sure I won't try and molest you," she says with a grin. Of course, the mention of her molesting me has my eyes lowering to the top of her corset where her breasts are spilling out. "Oh, right. Let me go change into my pajamas," she mutters when I'm caught staring.

"That's probably a good idea," I agree. While I'm not tempted to sleep with her, that doesn't mean I don't like looking at her curves.

Kelsey is an attractive woman, and any straight man would be lucky to have her.

CHAPTER 27

Lathan

I played like shit in Sunday's home game, my first full day as an unhappily married man. After dropping two easy catches when I was wide open down the field, Coach took me out and put in my backup. I fucking hated it, but I can't say I blamed him.

My head just wasn't out there with me in the stadium. Or maybe it was my heart that felt like it was missing. Saturday night when Kelsey and I finally laid down, both of us clothed in our normal non-sexy pajamas, I just couldn't sleep. I kept thinking about Pax. How angry he was and that I wish he would've just given me a chance to explain.

Today, four days later, I'm freezing my ass off on the practice field. Behind my thin gloves made for catching balls and not for warmth, my fingers feel like they could snap right off. There's a chance of snow tonight. So, with the temperature dropping, the frozen footballs Quinton is throwing come at me like unrelenting bullets, likely leaving bruises underneath my pads.

"Savage!"

When Coach Griffin shouts my name from across the sidelines, I know he's about to chew my ass out for playing shitty again. But when I yank my helmet off and turn around to jog over to him, my cleats nearly trip me up when I see Kelsey standing beside our head coach. She's all bundled up in a big, white coat with a pink hat pulled down over her ears, her arms around herself, looking absolutely miserable in the cold. As I get closer and see her sad brown eyes on me, I begin to get the feeling that the look on her face doesn't have anything to do with the weather.

"Hey," I say when I'm standing in front of her. Remembering that this is my new wife I'm supposed to be head over heels in love with, I toss my helmet to the grass and wrap her in my arms for a hug. "What are you doing here?" I whisper in her ear as she squeezes me back tightly around my waist.

"I'm so sorry, Lathan," she murmurs into my chest. "It's your mom..."

"My mom?" I exclaim, pulling back to see her face. "What about her?" I ask. This morning she was supposed to start her chemo treatments again.

"Your dad called the house when he couldn't get you on your cell phone," Kelsey explains with tears filling her eyes. "She was running a fever and too weak for treatment. They had to admit her."

"She's in the hospital?" I ask in confusion. "But she was doing so good...how...I don't understand."

"Your dad said you should hurry. So, if you want to get changed, I'll drive you to the hospital," she offers.

"He said that?" I ask her. "For me to hurry?"

Kelsey nods.

Fuck, it must be bad. Usually, my dad assures me everything is fine, that he's taking care of mom and for me to focus on practice or the game coming up. He *never* insists that I rush home.

"Coach, I'm sorry..." I start when I look over to him, but he waves me off.

"Go. Get out of here. That's an order," he says, pointing toward the locker rooms.

"I'll meet you in the parking lot," I tell Kelsey before I sprint inside the building to get changed.

A few minutes later, we're on the road. Neither Kelsey nor I say a word as she drives as fast as safely possible up the highway. She's already programmed the address for Elon Memorial in her phone, so the navigation's occasional robotic voice is the only sound for nearly three hours.

I called my dad to tell him we were on the way, but he didn't say much, just that he'll see us then.

"Can I go in with you?" Kelsey speaks up and asks when we turn into the hospital.

"Yeah, of course," I tell her. "And thanks for driving me."

"That's what wives do," she says, flashing me a sad smile before we get parked.

A man sitting at the hospital's registration desk tells us which room Mom's in. And after a short ride up the elevator to the third floor, we're there.

Her room is dark, with only a dim light on at the head of her bed. She's sleeping peacefully under the white sheets, not a single cord or plug surrounding her like most hospital visits. And my dad is sitting on the edge of the bed beside her, holding her hand with his head hung.

"Dad?" I ask, needing him to tell me what the hell is going on.

"Lathan, hey, you made it," he says when he gets to his feet and grabs tissues from the dispenser on the bed tray.

"How is she? What happened?" I ask, looking at mom, who hasn't even blinked her eyes open since we walked in. When my dad comes over and hugs me, I feel his shoulders shaking before I hear his sobs.

"We're losing her," he says between sniffles. "The doctors...the doctors don't even think there's time to call...to call hospice in."

That's all he's able to say before he breaks down completely, and I can't hold myself together any longer.

No, no, no. This can't be happening! Mom was supposed to start getting treatments and getting better, dammit! Maybe the doctors are wrong and she's just tired. With some rest, she could wake up feeling better...

When my dad finally lets go of me a few minutes later, he says, "I'll give you a few minutes while I go to the bathroom to clean up."

"Okay," I agree, barely able to speak that one word.

"Can I get you anything, Mr. Savage? Maybe some coffee or...or some water?" Kelsey asks.

"A bottle of water would be great, sweetheart," he says, wrapping an arm around her shoulders as they leave the room to give me time alone with Mom. "I'll show you where the vending machines are."

I grab my own pile of tissues to dry my face and blow my nose before I take a seat next to her on the bed. Reaching for her small, dainty hand, I hold it in mine, my heart breaking at how cold and frail it feels.

"Mom?" I say, my voice cracking. "Mom, can you hear me? This wasn't supposed to happen. Not so...so soon..."

Tears pour down my cheeks as I lean down over her chest and hold her. The beating of her heart is so slow and weak that I barely feel it.

"I love you," I tell her as I cry on her. "I love you....and... and I don't know what I'll do without you."

My sobs are so loud that I almost miss her soft whisper, my mother telling me the last words I'll ever hear her say.

"I love you too, baby."

CHAPTER 28

Pax

Slouching down in one of the seats in the family box at the Wildcats stadium, I cram one end of my hotdog into my mouth, barely even chewing it as we wait for the game to start.

"Slow down before you choke," Roxy's old man warns me from his usual seat next to mine.

"I'm hungry," I mutter around the huge bite while I chew it up.

"Yeah, so am I, but at least I have some manners," he argues, dabbing his napkin over his white mustache that's even lighter than his hair.

"Oh, how I've missed these fun conversations of ours," I tease since he wasn't able to make it to the last few games because of his college team's schedule. I do like hanging out with Mr. Benson. He's a cool old guy.

"How's my girl been doing? We've both been so busy I've hardly heard from her over the past two weeks," he says.

"Roxy's good," I assure him. "Kohen and her are so sickeningly lovey dovey I can't tolerate them for long periods of time."

"You've been around them more than I have. Is Kohen good to her?" he asks.

"Yeah, he is," I reply honestly. "If he weren't, he would be in a wheelchair with two broken legs."

"Got that right. One from me and one from you," her dad says, offering me a fist bump.

"Fuck yeah," I agree as I hit it.

"So what about you?" Mr. Benson asks. "Any special men in your life?"

"Uh-uh. Nope. Nada," I reply before cramming more dog into my mouth.

"Eh, I'm sure one will come along soon enough," he says, right as the stadium announcer's deep voice rumbles through the PA system, welcoming the fans.

It's too bad that I thought one special man had come along until it all went to hell.

I haven't spoken to Lathan in over a week, not since right before his wedding, and he hasn't even tried to contact me to explain. Which is probably my fault for telling him we were done the last time we spoke. That was before my conversation with his mother, though.

My mind is still blown wondering if he got married just because of her sickness or if he was too scared to come out of the closet. I mean, if he wanted to give her a wedding, why couldn't the two of us have just tied the knot?

Okay, so that's probably unrealistic and an unfair thing to ask of Lathan, to go from right out of the closet to marrying a man, but still. Why didn't he just tell me what was going on? And, based on the text message he sent me the morning of his wedding about seeing me later, did he really expect us to keep messing around with each other *after* he had a wife as if nothing had changed?

Fuck that.

"Here they come," Roxy's dad says, nudging my arm with his elbow before he gets to his feet like all the other friends and family in the box and most of the fans in the stadium.

I shove the last bite of my hotdog into my mouth, wipe my ketchup and mustard hands on a napkin, and stand up to clap along with the crowd.

The smoke and pyrotechnics start going off at the tunnel entrance before each name of the offensive line is called. One player at a time they come running out to near-deafening applause.

Only when the announcer starts announcing the defense do I realize they didn't say Lathan's name. And there's no way I could have missed it.

Is he hurt? Did he get in trouble with his coach? Why isn't he starting today?

He did get pulled out of the game last week, so maybe his backup is starting.

The last of the players are announced, and then the rest of the team runs out onto the field. I keep looking for Lathan's number eighty-six jersey, but he's not down there on the field or the sidelines.

That's when the announcer's voice booms through the stadium, "As we all grieve for the sad loss of the mother of our teammate, please stand for a moment of silence, honoring the memory of Mrs. Debra Savage. May Lathan and his family be in your thoughts and prayers during this difficult time. The Wildcats organization will be making a donation to the American Cancer Society in Mrs. Savage's name, and we hope you will consider doing the same."

"What?" I exclaim, causing Roxy's dad to shush me as everyone bows their head in silent prayer.

Lathan just lost his mom to cancer? The sweet lady from the wedding is gone?

Why didn't anyone fucking tell me? I can't help but wonder as my chest seizes up and I can't seem to get any air.

Oh. Right.

Because no one knows about us.

God, I can't imagine what Lathan is going through, how difficult this must be for him. Married or not, I need to see him, to tell him how sorry I am and make sure he's okay. Although, I doubt he's okay. How could he be?

"Now, please remove your hats for our national anthem," the announcer instructs the thousands of people gathered in the stadium.

"I've got to go," I tell Mr. Benson. "Let Roxy know I'm sorry and that I'll call her later?" I ask him.

"Ah, yeah, sure," he turns and says to me with a furrowed brow. "Everything okay?"

"No," I reply. "No, it's not."

...

A few hours later, after doing an address search for Debra Savage on my phone, I'm standing in front of a cute, little, two-story brick home, a solemn white wreath hanging on the door. I don't see Lathan's Jeep, but there are a ton of cars parked in the driveway and along the curb, so I assume he must be here.

What if he doesn't want to see me? We didn't exactly part on great terms last week.

I nearly chicken out, turn around and drive back to Wilmington. But then I remind myself the reason I drove straight here. I came to offer my condolences to a man I still care for, and I'm not leaving until I do it.

Raising my hand, I finally press the button for the doorbell and suck in a deep breath while straightening my suit jacket as I wait. Good thing I wore my usual crisp suit to the stadium like usual or I would feel underdressed right now.

When the door opens, it's the last person I was expecting to see standing on the other side.

"Paxton!" the woman who married the man I love says, her brown eyes widening in surprise. Then she shocks the shit out of me when she throws her arms around my neck to hug me like we're old friends. "I'm glad you're here. Lathan will be so happy to see you," she says softly while I stand frozen in surprise because of her embrace.

Did I fall down a rabbit hole or land in the Twilight Zone?

How the fuck does Lathan's wife know who I am? And why the hell does she seem so excited to see me?

"Um, hi," I eventually say as I tentatively pat her back in return.

"Come on in," she says when she lets me go. "I'm Kelsey, by the way."

"Right," I reply as she grabs my hand and leads me inside where a dozen or more people are standing around or sitting in the cozy living room, all speaking softly to each other.

"Let me take you back to Lathan's room so you two can have some privacy," Kelsey whispers while pulling me down a hallway.

We end up in a bedroom full of football memorabilia, trophies, and awards. "I'll go get Lathan and be right back," she tells me before she disappears.

Still confused by her odd friendliness, I pace around the queen size bed nervously, looking at the various photos on the wall until I hear the door shut and his voice behind me.

"Pax?"

Turning around, I hadn't prepared myself for the sight of Lathan after a week, or the weight of sadness that's not only obvious in his stormy gray eyes but written all over his face.

"Hey," I reply, shoving my hands into my pants pockets nervously. "I'm really sorry, Lathan. I just heard –"

That's the last word I get out before he launches himself at me, nearly knocking me over with the force of his embrace since my hands are still in my pockets. As I free them to return his hug, I'm instantly relieved because he didn't tell me to leave after I was such a jerk to him the last time we saw each other. Then, my heart begins to break when his body shakes from his devastation.

"I'm sorry," I tell him over and over as I hold him to me, meaning for everything.

We stand there for a long time in each other's arms before I lead him over to sit down beside me on the edge of the bed. Even then I still don't let him go but keep my arm around him.

"Can I do anything? Do you need anything?" I ask him while he pulls up the front of his tee to wipe off his face.

Shaking his head, he says, "No. Everything is done for tomorrow, just have to talk to all the people who keep coming by..."

"Oh, yeah. That must suck," I tell him. Then it occurs to me that *I'm* one of those people dropping in on him while he's just trying to grieve. "I should probably get out of here, leave you alone," I say.

"No. Stay. I wasn't talking about you," Lathan replies while grasping onto my forearm. "I meant my parents' friends and neighbors. People from our church. They come by to bring us food, which is great and all, but then they just hang out and talk when I don't feel like fucking talking."

"You don't have to talk to anyone," I tell him. "Screw them all. Just stay here and hide from them if you want. They won't mind."

"I know, I wish I could, but I'm trying to take some of the pressure off my dad," he explains. "Just stay with me for a little while?"

"Yeah, however long you want," I tell him, pulling his head to my shoulder to stroke his short hair.

After several long minutes, he says, "It's my fault for putting too much stress on her with the wedding. I shouldn't have rushed things."

My jaw clenches tight hearing the weight of unnecessary guilt in his voice.

"No, Lathan. You can't blame yourself. She had cancer, right? That's what happened to her," I assure him.

Shaking his head against me, he says, "Dad said she was exhausted afterward and couldn't get out of bed. It's my fault. I was a fucking idiot..."

"No, you weren't. And the cancer is what was wearing her down. Not you or the...wedding," I say, hesitating over that last word because I hate it so much in this particular context.

"I feel so guilty and lost," he says against my chest while still clutching me. "I had no idea how hard this would be."

"I can't imagine," I say as I hold him tighter.

While I may not be close with my parents, my Nana jumped in and filled both of their roles ten years ago. Honestly, I don't know what I would do if something happened to her. Each year she gets a little older, and I worry her time is running out. She's the only family I have now.

Clearing his throat, Lathan pulls away from me and suddenly gets to his feet. "I should probably get back out there. Sorry I'm such a mess," he says as he swipes his fingers under each of his red, swollen eyes that are surrounded by dark circles.

"You don't have to apologize for anything," I tell him from my seat on the bed. "And don't take this the wrong way, but when was the last time you slept?'

"Not more than a few hours the past few nights. Just too much on my mind, you know?" he says.

"Then why don't you take something to try and help you rest?" I suggest. "Tomorrow's the funeral, right?"

"Yeah," he answers with a jerk of his head.

"So, you need to rest up, because tomorrow is going to be even more stressful and difficult."

"I can't leave my dad alone..." he starts.

"Go say hello to everyone here, see if your dad needs anything; and if not, then will you take a sleeping pill?" I ask.

Scrubbing his palms down his face, he considers it for a moment before he tells me, "Fine. I feel like I'm about to fall over anyway."

Getting to my feet, I give his shoulder a supportive squeeze and tell him, "Good. I know you're worried about your dad, but you can't forget to take care of yourself too."

Looking down at me with his pitiful, stormy, red-rimmed eyes, he asks, "Will you stay with me? Here? Tonight?"

With a groan that I can't prevent, I let my hand fall from him and say, "I don't know, Lathan. How do you think your wife would feel about that? Not to mention your dad with everything else he has going on..."

"Kelsey won't mind. She's been sleeping in the spare bedroom the last few nights, and she knows about you."

My jaw falls open and hits the carpet. "What do you mean she *knows* about me?"

Using his tongue to wet his lips, he says, "She knows about us. And she agreed to marry me as a favor because my parents thought I was engaged after my mom found Quinton's ring for Callie. Mom was so excited that I couldn't bear to disappoint her by telling her it wasn't mine..."

"Oh," I mutter in shock that he told someone about the two of us, everything about the two of us. "So, you haven't...slept with Kelsey or anything?"

"No," he answers right away. "I mean, the night we got married she wanted to, but I couldn't."

He hasn't fucked her but he could have.

I don't even know what to say to that.

"So, will you stay?" he asks.

"Of course," I tell him.

"Thank you," he replies with an exhale. "Get comfortable, and I'll, ah, be back in a few minutes. Hopefully."

"I'll be here," I tell him, meaning that in every way as he goes over to open the door and leave.

While Lathan may not be in a loving marriage, and although he's been honest with Kelsey about us, that doesn't mean he and I can go back to how things were. I just don't think we can really be together until he's ready to come out. It'll be too hard otherwise, the constant hiding, sneaking around. Lathan will always be worried about someone outing us, and it will eventually ruin everything good we could have. And it would be good. I'm almost certain of it.

But that's not what tonight is about, and I don't plan to get into any of that with him here while he's mourning his mother. Besides, it's not like I even know whether or not he still wants to be with me.

As I wait for Lathan to return, I take off my suit jacket and hang it on the back of a computer chair at his childhood desk and remove my shoes too. Then, I spend the rest of the time looking through the various awards and photos in his room. In the first photo, one of a football team that I assume was from during high school; it takes me forever to pick out Lathan from the rows of uniforms. Wow. I had no idea he was such a big guy and likely a lineman. Over the various years of pictures he has hanging up, he's the same size in all of them.

"Oh, fuck," Lathan says when he slips back into the room silently. "I should've told you *not* to look at anything while I was gone."

Straightening from the photo I'm currently on, I tell him, "I had no idea you were..."

"Enormous? Yeah, I was, until the middle of college. High school was hell."

"Guess that explains the shyness," I tell him as I face him again. "Do you know why I wear suits?"

"Because you're a gigolo?" Lathan answers, repeating what I said when I was joking with him the night of his first blowjob in the restaurant bathroom. There's even a hint of a smile on his sad, weary face.

"Because I took a lot of shit after I came out. And then in college, when I played football with Roxy, our coach would make us dress up for away games. He said it instills a sense of confidence in each of us and the team as a group. Then I realized that when I dressed nice, I actually gained some level of respect from everyone, and I liked how that felt, so I wanted that all of the time. As crazy as it sounds, the suits make me feel like I have public approval, even if I don't."

"That doesn't sound crazy at all," Lathan replies, his words trailing off on a yawn. "Sorry."

"You need to rest. Did you find any meds to take?" I ask, watching as he pulls his shirt over his head but trying not to ogle his chest and six-pack abs. I fail horribly, because I am only human and he's...a masterpiece.

"Yeah, my mom had…I found some Nyquil in the cabinet," Lathan says, causing my chest to squeeze when he pauses after the mention of her. Clearing his throat, he keeps undressing down to his boxer briefs as he tells me, "There's plenty of food in the kitchen if you get hungry."

"I'm fine," I assure him. "Have you eaten anything?" I ask in concern.

"Oh yeah," he answers. "Comfort food has always been my go-to for stress and shit. The problem is making myself *stop* eating."

"You can eat all you want if it helps," I assure him as he lifts the covers and climbs in bed.

"Right now I just want you to get in here with me so I can try to sleep for more than an hour," he says, patting the empty side of the bed.

"Should I…is it okay if I take off my shirt and pants?" I ask before I remove them.

"Yeah, get comfortable. Most everyone out front has left, so my dad said he's gonna turn off the porch light. It works to stop trick-or-treaters on Halloween, so maybe it will work the same on well-meaning grievers."

"Hopefully," I agree, unbuttoning my dress shirt to remove it. I also have a white undershirt on, but I take it off too, wanting the skin-to-skin contact tonight with Lathan even if neither of us is in the mood for more than cuddles and sleep. Pausing with my hand on the fly of my pants, I ask, "Are you sure your dad is okay with me staying here? I don't want to cause any problems with what he already has going on here."

"I told him that my friend Pax is staying tonight and that I would introduce you in the morning," Lathan answers. "Now quit procrastinating and come get in bed."

"Yes, sir," I agree with a smile as I step out of my pants and go around the bed to crawl in next to him.

As soon as I'm beside Lathan, stretched out on my back, he

throws an arm over my waist and curls his body around mine. "I've missed you," he says softly.

"Why didn't you call me, or hell, why didn't you tell me about her weeks ago..." I ask him.

"I thought we were just fucking around," he mutters, making me cringe. He didn't think that what we had constituted more than fuck buddies. "And then after...well, I wasn't sure if you were still angry with me."

"Even if I were, I would've still been here," I tell him, resting my chin on the top of his head, breathing in his comforting, familiar scent and soaking up as much of his warmth as possible in case this is the last chance I get. "Now get some sleep," I order.

CHAPTER 29

Lathan

The funeral service was nice. The strange thing was that no one, not even my dad and especially not Preacher Roberts who did the sermon, seemed entirely surprised by my mom's death. Everyone just...sadly accepts it.

She had cancer. The oncologists couldn't get rid of it. So, she died.

It seems so simple to all of her friends and family members, but not to me. Maybe because I wasn't ready to admit that she wasn't capable of beating the sickness. I kept throwing money at the problem, hoping it could buy a cure when it obviously couldn't.

I'm probably an idiot for remaining so optimistic for this long. As Eric Clapton's song, "Tears in Heaven", plays through the sound system of the same church I was married in a little more than a week ago, I can't help but wonder if I would've been better off preparing for the worst instead of hoping for the best.

And while I watch the pallbearers carry my mother's cherry wood casket to the hearse waiting just outside the doors, I can't stop thinking how lucky I was to have had a woman so loving and kind in my life when Pax's parents couldn't accept who he was. She was the best mother anyone could ask for, and now she's gone, taken from me and my dad way too soon.

Since I first saw Pax last night, it's felt like some of the heavy weight of the past few nightmarish days has been lifted off my shoulders. After my mom passed, I can't help but wonder what she would've said if she had known about Pax and me. Because even as religious as my parents are, I just can't see my mom abandoning me for anything, especially not for who I loved. Which makes me feel... awful for lying to her.

I should've just told both of my parents the truth. If no one else in the world would've accepted the real me, wouldn't they have and been happy that I found someone?

Instead, the last memories I gave my mother were big, fat lies, and I regret them. Not just because I wasn't honest with my parents; but as my dad, Kelsey and I walk past the rows of loved ones, and I momentarily lock eyes with Paxton, I know I'm mostly disappointed that I was too scared to be honest with myself.

...

Pax

Kelsey may not be his actual wife who Lathan loves, but I'm still jealous of her. During the funeral and the graveside service, she's been able to stick by his side, holding his hand, rubbing his back, offering him support during the darkest days of his life while all I can do is look at him and sympathize from afar.

I fucking hate it.

I want to be the one next to him, comforting him. And I can't stand seeing him hurting like this. If I could take his pain away from him and make it mine, I would, because I love him that much...

For the first time in my life, I love another man. And what good is it doing me? None whatsoever. Lathan and I are not together now, and there are no plans for a relationship in the future. He's a married professional football player, and I'm...nothing but his secret affair.

Love apparently doesn't conquer all.

Even so, that's why after the service is over, I don't immediately leave to drive back to Wilmington. Instead, I go with the rest of his friends to the Savages' house. Mostly, I just want the chance to have a moment alone with Lathan and make sure he's okay, or at least as okay as one can possibly be after saying goodbye to the mother he loved dearly.

"I'm surprised you came," Roxy says when she sidles up to where I'm standing with my back against the wall in the hallway. I was hoping Lathan would walk by and we could sneak into his room to talk. So far that hasn't happened. "When exactly did you get here?" my best friend, who knows me better than anyone in the world, asks with a raised blonde eyebrow.

"A few hours ago," I lie, lowering my eyes. I hate lying to Roxy, but I just can't tell her that I left the game yesterday to come up here, or that I ended up spending the night with Lathan.

"Where did you go yesterday during the game?" she prods, giving me the third degree because she's suspicious and she's probably upset because she knows I'm keeping something from her.

"I was sick. Damn stadium hot dogs," I tell her. "Never learn my lesson."

"You look fine now," Roxy points out. "No, actually you don't look fine. You look miserable like *you* just lost someone you loved when you never even met Lathan's mother. I didn't know you were so tender hearted..."

"I did meet her," I say before I can shove the words back down my throat. "Leave it alone, Roxy," I warn her when her lips part as if to comment further.

And she doesn't get a chance to say anything else before the big, graying man I recognize as Lathan's father walks up to us.

"Thank you, kids, for coming," he says, placing a hand on Roxy's shoulder. "I know it means a lot for Lathan to have his teammates' support," he tells her and then lifts his somber blue eyes to me. "I recognized the Wildcats only female player right away but not you. Do you play?"

"Ah, no," I reply, glancing at Roxy and back to Lathan's dad. Rather than comment that I'm the one who stayed with Lathan last night, I tell him, "I'm just Roxy's best friend."

"This is Paxton Price," Roxy introduces us.

Mr. Savage's brow crinkles as he holds out his hand for me to shake, which I, of course, take. "Pax," he confirms. Does he remember Lathan telling him about me last night? Is he gonna mention me spending the night in front of Roxy? Oh fuck.

"I'm so sorry for your loss," I tell him sincerely, hoping to stem off either scenario.

"Thanks for being here for Lathan," he says. "He needs as many...friends as he can get right now."

"It was nice to meet you, and again my condolences," I tell him before he walks off down the hall.

"They've had a stressful day," Roxy says. "Let's go find Lathan and say goodbye."

"Yeah, okay," I agree, even if I'm not ready to leave him or pretend I barely know him in front of everyone else.

When we find him talking to a gaggle of white-haired women, he quickly thanks us for coming and tells Kohen, Roxy and me bye. I don't even get to hug him one last time. He simply shakes my hand and turns back to the old women.

CHAPTER 30

Lathan

"Are you sure you don't need me to stay?" I ask my dad the day after mom's funeral. It seems too soon to bail on him, but Kelsey is in her car out front, waiting for me to say goodbye.

"Son, I know you feel like you need to be here, but your team needs you more. And you've seen the foot traffic through this house the last few days. There will be *plenty* of people checking in on me."

"I wish I lived closer," I tell him, feeling guilty that practices and games will keep me away from now until close to Christmas.

"You're following your dream, and that requires sacrifices. Don't ever feel bad about that," he says, giving me a hug that ends with a slap to my back. "I'm proud of you, and I want to see you on the field, not here. Hey, I can even come to your games now."

After several hours of keeping my shit together, the tightly sealed cork pops off the top of all those bottled down emotions and I lose it with the reminder that Mom won't ever be cheering me on again, not from the stadium or from home...

My dad clutches me in another hug. And when I hear him sniffling, I feel a little better knowing I'm not the only one.

"Now get on the road. Keep yourself busy. That's what I plan to do," Dad says when he pulls away and wipes his face with the sleeve of his Wildcats Henley.

"Yeah, okay. I'll try," I say, using the sleeves of my hoodie to dry up my own eyes. Then I heft the duffle, which Kelsey thoughtfully packed before she picked me up at the stadium last week, onto my shoulder.

"Oh, wait!" Dad exclaims. "I found something for you. It was in your Mom's purse when I was looking for her checkbook this morning," he says. "Let me grab it." He disappears into the kitchen and returns with a white envelope. When he hands it to me, I see my name written in her blue cursive on the front. "I didn't open it, so I don't know what it says."

"Thanks," I tell him, swallowing around the boulder that's suddenly lodged in my throat. "I'll open it when I get home," I say since I'm afraid I'll get too upset right now and cry all the way back.

"Whenever you're ready," he says. "Have a safe trip and call me when you get home."

"I will," I agree, stepping forward for another quick one-armed embrace before I leave.

"Love you, son."

"Love you too," I say, turning around and pushing through the front door to escape before I become a sloppy, crying mess again.

After I toss my bag in the backseat of her little Toyota and sit down in the front passenger seat with the envelope still clutched in my hand, Kelsey asks, "Are you sure you're ready to go back? If you want to stay longer, I can come get you in a few days..."

"Nah, I've got to get back to practice, and Dad said he's fine," I tell her as I buckle up.

"Whatcha got?" she asks, nodding to the letter before backing out of the driveway.

"It's from my mom," I say.

"Oh, wow," Kelsey replies, keeping her eyes on the road.

"I'll open it when we get home," I tell her, patting the stationary against my knee that's bouncing uncontrollably.

The truth is I'm torn.

Part of me can't wait to tear into it, while the other part wants to keep it like it is, sealed up, because this is it. After I read what's inside, there's nothing else left of my mother but photos, a few home movies, and my happy memories. This will be the last thing she ever says to me, and I'm not ready to face that yet. I am curious to see what it says, though, so I'll open it, and probably soon.

"So, when we get back, I'll start packing up," Kelsey says. It takes me several seconds to remember that she moved in with me right after the wedding. All of that seems like a lifetime ago.

"Are you sure?" I ask her. "I mean, what will everyone else say if we're no longer living together right after the funeral?"

"Oh, so you want me to stay?" Kelsey asks, glancing over quickly at me before her eyes go back to the road.

"Yeah, I mean, unless you don't want to," I reply. "Honestly, I don't even know what I want. Can you just stay until things calm down?" I ask. "I don't want to deal with all the questions from people on top of everything else..."

"Sure," she answers. "I can stay."

"Good, thanks," I tell her.

On the rest of the drive home, I think of the other main reason I want her to stay and keep up the appearance that we're a couple.

I want to be with Pax now that he knows the truth and see if we can pick things back up to start seeing each other again. With Kelsey going along with the marriage a little longer, that wouldn't give anyone a reason to suspect he and I are together.

...

A few hours later when Kelsey and I get home, before I even unpack, I'm not able to wait any longer. I sit down on the sofa and pull out the letter from the envelope. Another tri-folded piece of paper falls into my lap. When I unfold it, I realize it's my and Kelsey's marriage license. After the ceremony, my mom and Kelsey's mother signed as our witnesses. Then, Preacher Roberts was supposed to fill out his part and mail it back to the Register of Deeds for us. So what the hell was my mom doing with that? Hopefully, her letter will explain so I dive in and start reading.

Dear Lathan,

I don't know how I can ever tell you how much I love you. There are not enough words in the world to explain what you mean to me. I only wish I had more time to see you continue to become a man I greatly admire and respect.

Your wedding was so beautiful, and getting to be part of it made me feel hopeful for the first time since I was diagnosed. It reminded me that even though I may not always be there for you, there are so many other people who love and care for you. But still, it was selfish of me not to try harder to convince you to call it off.

While Kelsey is a beautiful, lovely girl, I'm not convinced that she's the person you belong with. That's why I couldn't in good conscience let your marriage become official. I asked Preacher Roberts to give the enclosed license to me after the wedding instead of sending it to be filed at the courthouse. If I was wrong, you can still do so. If I'm right, then what are you waiting for, baby? Be with the person who makes you happy.

Life is too short not to spend every day with the one you love. It may not always be easy, but it's worth it. I'm just so happy that I was able to meet him. You should be too.

Love,
Mom

Oh, my God.

My mom met Pax at the wedding?

But most importantly, she knew and she was okay with the two of us? For days now I've regretted not being honest with her, but it didn't matter. She knew and she approved, which is the best news I've had in a really long time.

...

Pax

"Hey," Lathan says when I open the door for him late Tuesday night.

"Hey," I say in surprise. "You're back."

"Yeah, and I need to talk to you."

"Ah, sure," I say, opening the door for him to come in.

Once it's closed, shutting out the rest of the world again, Lathan steps forward and winds his arms around me. His damp lips kissing my jaw nearly make my knees go weak before I remove his hands from my hips and release them. Then, I take a step back to put space between us.

"We can't," I tell him, stabbing my fingers through my hair because I want his mouth on me, but I'm trying to remember all the reasons that I told myself we shouldn't. "Lathan, I know you're going through a really rough time right now, and I'll always be here for you, but only as your friend."

"I'm not legally married," he tells me.

"What does that mean?" I ask in confusion.

From his back jeans pocket, Lathan pulls out a sheet of paper and holds it up in front of him before he tears it in halves and then quarters.

"My mom got a hold of the marriage license that the preacher was supposed to file to make it official. She knew about you and said she met you."

"Yeah, um, she did. The day of the wedding. After you left," I admit.

"I didn't know that," he says. "But now, well, Kelsey knows that we're not legally married, but she's still willing to pretend to keep up appearances and all. That means that you and I could finally be together..."

"No, Lathan. It doesn't work like that," I tell him. "We'll still have to sneak around, and you'll always wonder if someone is gonna find out. I can't live like that, and I don't think you can either."

"So, you don't want to be with me?" he asks, his stormy gray eyes boring a hole right through me.

"Not that way," I reluctantly declare. "I came out ten years ago because I was tired of the secrets. I was tired of hiding a part of me. My nightclub is about to open, and there's no way I'm going back to that life. I love you, but you can't ask me to do that," I tell him.

When his lips part and his gray eyes widen I realize what I've just said.

"You...you love me?" he asks.

Clearing the emotion from my throat, with my hands on my hips, I say, "Yes, which is why I need more from you than a secret affair."

"You know I can't do that, Pax!" he replies. "And if you love me, then you would want to be with me in any way possible."

"I'm sorry, Lathan," I tell him honestly. "I'm sorry that you lost your mother, and I'm sorry that you can't give me what I need. I understand that you're not ready to face the consequences, but that doesn't mean I deserve to be the runner-up to anyone, even your fake wife."

"I just..." he starts before turning his back to me. "I wish I could change your mind."

"I wish you could too," I admit. "We can still be friends..."

"Fuck you and fuck your friendship," he shouts over his shoulder. "You and I both know that will never work, so fuck you!"

After using his favorite phrase when he's angry, he storms over and wrenches open the door.

"Why don't you just go home and fuck your fake wife already? You know you want to," I yell back at him, angry at him for not having the balls to come out and angry at myself for not having to be with him any way possible. And yeah, because I'm jealous of her and can't help but wonder if he wants her.

"You're right. I should," Lathan snaps. "Maybe I'll even like pussy better, which would save me a helluva lot of trouble."

"Sure, hide your cock in her while you keep lying to yourself!" I shout just as Lathan slams the door behind him and leaves on that wonderful note.

Dammit. I hate myself for saying that shit and for hurting him. For a second, I almost consider giving in and going after him because I tell myself that having Lathan in my life whatever way I can get it is better than nothing.

But I know that's not true.

The scenario he wants only includes having him in my bed a few nights a week when I want more.

I want all of his nights and all of his days too.

CHAPTER 31

Lathan

As soon as I get home, I go straight to the liquor cabinet. I'm not sure which is worse, binge eating or drinking, but for right now I just want to be drunk. Food can't make me forget Pax and the alcohol can, or at least it will make the details of him fuzzy for a little while.

"Hey, are you okay?" Kelsey asks when she appears in the kitchen.

I don't even bother with a glass; I just unscrew the lid and drink straight from the first bottle I pick up.

"I'm fine," I tell her after I swallow a mouthful and wipe my mouth on the back of my hand.

"People who are fine don't usually guzzle vodka like that," she points out.

When I turn around to say something snarky back to her, I find her leaning a shoulder against the wall with her arms crossed over her chest. A chest that's only covered by the thin white cotton of a spaghetti strap tank top, no bra. My dick twitches in my jeans, liking the view of her hard nipples, *a lot*, definitely proving that I'm not gay. I could fuck Kelsey right here, right now on the counter if I wanted. And she would let me.

Fuck. What the hell am I even thinking!

Pax was right; even if I sleep with Kelsey, it doesn't change anything, especially not the fact that I'll still want to be with him. That I'll still love him.

"Did you have a fight with Pax?" Kelsey asks. "I thought he would be happy we aren't officially married."

"Yeah, he doesn't care. We're done," I tell her, chugging from the bottle. "But that's not what I want. I'm not ready to give up even though I can't give him what he needs..."

"I'm sorry," she says. Coming over she stands on her tippy toes to give me a kiss on the cheek. "I wish I could be what you need."

"I appreciate that," I reply honestly. "But right now, I don't think I can even pretend we're together anymore."

"You want me to leave?" she asks in understanding.

"Yeah, I think that might be best," I agree with a nod. "And if anyone asks, you can tell them I'm a huge dick that you can't stand to be around."

Kelsey gives me a small smile and says, "That's not true. Even if it was, I would never say that. Since the license was never filed, how about we just stick with the story that we may have rushed things and we decided to get an annulment, if anyone asks?"

"That sounds good," I agree, giving her a hug. "Thanks for putting up with me."

"You're welcome. And just so you know, I donated all the money your attorney's given me to the American Cancer Society."

"Ugh, you're the best," I tell her, placing a kiss on the top of her head. "It's a shame I had to fall in love with a man."

"No, a shame would be if you didn't try to work things out with Pax," she says before pulling away.

CHAPTER 32

Pax

"Can I stay with you tonight?" I ask Roxy over the phone as I lie face down on my bed. "Or would Kohen let you come have a sleepover?"

"Sure, I can come over," she says. "What's wrong?"

"Everything," I mutter.

"I'm on my way," she replies before hanging up.

A few minutes later, Roxy lets herself into the house with the key I gave her and finds me still in the same position --- face buried in pillows.

"What happened, Pax?" she asks as she climbs on the bed and stretches out next to me. When she throws her arm over my back, our faces are only a few inches apart. "You haven't lived here long enough to have your heart broken."

"Actually, I have," I tell her.

"Guy from back home?"

"Nope."

"New guy here?"

"Yep."

"Aww, I'm sorry. He's the new closet case?" she guesses.

"Yep. Isn't that always the case?" I ask.

"I know it sucks, but just think of all the hot, openly gay men you'll get to meet at your club," she says optimistically.

"Yeah, but I don't want any of them," I whine. "I want the closet case."

"I'm sorry it didn't work out. Again," she replies with a pouty lip sticking out.

"Am I crazy for telling him I don't want to sneak around because he can't come out? I mean, am I the asshole here?"

"No, of course not," she tells me. "Kohen and I had to hide our relationship, and it sucked. If this guy can't give you what you need, then you shouldn't have to compromise."

"I know. But why does that decision feel so shitty?" I ask her.

"Because you miss him. It'll get better, though. Plenty of other men in the sea."

"What if he's the one, though, and I threw him back? I mean, I named my club after him, and who am I kidding? It's probably going to be a huge flop..."

"*He's* Moby Dick?" Roxy asks, green eyes wide in surprise. "I thought you named it after yourself."

"Nope. For him, and he won't ever even step foot inside of it."

"Maybe he will. He could always change his mind," she argues.

"I believed Oliver would leave his wife, and that never happened. This man I'm certain will never leave his...heterosexuality," I explain, almost spilling the beans when I mention Lathan's football contract.

"Then he doesn't deserve you," Roxy declares.

"I knew this would happen when I pursued him, and yet I did it anyway. Maybe I like making myself miserable."

"You deserve happiness and honesty, openness, and all the rest," she says confidently. "Don't even *think* of settling for anything less, Pax."

"Easy for you to say. You're with the man you love, and yet both of you still get to play football."

"Wait," Roxy says with a scrunched forehead. "What does football have to do with..." She gasps loudly before sitting up in bed. "He plays football?"

"No, I didn't say that," I respond quickly as I push myself up.

"Yes, you did. He can't come out because he's afraid of the fallout with teammates, the league, hell, all the fans..."

"No, Roxy. That's not what I meant. You're reaching..."

"You don't have to tell me who he is," she says. "But I have a guess. Ooh, a really good guess. Why you freaked out about Lathan and Kelsey getting married, why you drove all the way up to Elon for the funeral..."

"Please keep your mouth shut, especially to Kohen."

"Because he's our teammate! I knew it!" she exclaims, practically bouncing on the bed. "Is he the reason you moved here?"

"No, not really. I thought this was a great area for a club opening and you were here. Okay, maybe he had a tad to do with it because I wanted to pursue him."

"God, this seriously sucks, Pax," Roxy says as if I hadn't already figured that out.

"Yeah, it does, and I would do anything to fix it," I tell her sadly.

CHAPTER 33

Lathan

"Do either of you gentlemen need anything?" the peppy blonde flight attendant asks Quinton and me after our plane takes off from the away game we just won in Texas.

"No, thank you. I'm great," Quinton tells her politely with a smile.

Do I need anything?

Fuck, yes, I do.

It's been three weeks since I last saw Pax, and I'm so torn up I don't know which way is up and which is down. Between losing him and my mom, I've been a complete mess on and off the field. So many times I've nearly given in and called him, and once I even went to see him. He wasn't home, which made me go crazy wondering if he was with some other man...

"Sir, what about you? Do you need anything?" the attendant asks again.

"Yeah," I tell her. "Could you wave a magic wand and fix everything I've fucked up?" I ask, half-sloshed from three drinks at the hotel bar before we left. I am sober enough to notice that Quinton is staring at me like I've lost my mind.

"Ah, well, no. But I could get you a drink?" she replies with a friendly grin.

"A shot of Jager or the strongest shot you've got would be great," I tell her with a wink before she walks away.

"So, what's up with you?" Quinton asks. "You gave me back the engagement ring, but Kelsey's finger is still bare, so either you didn't buy another for her or she's refusing to wear it?"

"Huh?" I ask.

"Are you and Kelsey having problems?" he asks me point blank.

"Actually, we are," I admit. She's not Pax, so that's a pretty huge problem.

"Since that girl could get along with Hitler, you couldn't have been having arguments."

"Nope, no arguments," I agree just as the attendant hands me my shot that I throw back.

"Well, what's going on?" Quinton asks. "Are you having problems in the bedroom?"

I nearly spew my shot at that question before I force myself to swallow it.

"What? I have experience. Maybe I can give you some pointers," he says.

"I doubt you can help with this," I tell him.

"Try me. I've seen it all."

"No, I'm good," I reply while staring out the window and watching the clouds pass us by.

"Come on! I want to help. Whatever it is, you can tell me. Don't be embarrassed," he says.

Needing to tell someone before I explode, I blow out a breath and finally face him again.

"Quinton, I'm gay."

His blue eyes blink once while he remains silent. Then twice. By the third long blink, I'm starting to wish I would've kept my big ass mouth shut. Finally, I get a verbal response.

"Oh," he mutters before facing the front of the plane again and crossing his arms over his chest.

Oh? That's all the reaction I get from my best friend of four years. *Oh.* An expression used to convey surprise, shock, disappointment, sadness, any or all of the above.

"Well?" I prompt with my teeth ground together to prepare for his disgust.

"Well?" he repeats without facing me.

"Is that all you're going to say? *Oh*?" I ask.

"Excuse me for needing a moment to digest that piece of shocking information," he replies.

"You've had a moment. Lots of moments. Say something!" I demand so loudly that several of our teammates not wearing headphones turn to look at us.

"Does Kelsey know?" he asks softly, sounding pissed on her behalf.

"Yes, of course, she knows, since our wedding night –"

"You waited to tell her that on your honeymoon!" Quinton exclaims indignantly.

"Shhh," I warn him to keep it down. "Kelsey agreed to marry me because my mom saw the ring I was holding for you. Mom assumed it was mine and was so happy that I couldn't admit the truth. And I thought maybe she would agree to continue her treatment if she had something to look forward to."

"Oh," he mutters that annoying word again. "So, Kelsey knew all that?"

"Yes," I assure him, knowing he's a bit protective of his son's nanny. "Although I probably should've made it clear that nothing would happen between us since there was a misunderstanding after the wedding..."

"How long have you...I mean, have you known for a long time?" he asks.

"No. Not long. I was attracted to women, or so I thought, until..."

"Until what?"

"Until Pax."

"Pax!" he exclaims.

"Jesus fucking Christ, Quinton, why don't you just make a press release and tell the world already?" I groan, slumping further into my seat.

"Are you and him still..." he whispers.

"No, but only because I can't out myself in the league."

"Why not?" Quinton asks.

"Because I don't want to lose my contract," I state the obvious. "My parents...well, my parents depended on me to pay all my mom's medical bills." Guess that's no longer one of my reasons.

"Why do you think you would lose your contract?" he asks.

"Jeez, I dunno, Quinton. Maybe because none of the other guys would want me on the team with them."

"Why not?"

"Oh, my God," I mutter, slapping a hand over my face. "You know why; they'll all think I want them or whatever and that I'm looking at them in the shower..."

"Do you do that?" he whispers.

"No! Fuck no!" I shout. "It's not like that, at least not for me. I didn't even know I felt this way until Pax started messing with my head. He sent me gay porn..."

"You turned gay from watching gay porn?" Quinton gasps, clearly concerned that that's how it happens.

"No. Fuck, that's enough of this discussion," I tell him. "Just don't tell anyone, please?"

"Yeah, no, I won't," he agrees. "But I think you're wrong. It may not be that way."

"Sure," I grumble sarcastically. "I bet all the guys would throw rainbow confetti and give me a slap on the ass in congratulations when I tell them I like fucking a man."

"Whoa! TMI," Quinton says, holding up a palm to stop me from saying anything else. "Although, I think I always assumed that Pax would be a top..."

"Oh, he is," I agree.

"I was wrong," Quinton says while rubbing his forehead. "*That* was the TMI line you just crossed. Please don't give me any other specifics."

"No problem," I reply with a grin since it's sort of fun making the former sex God cringe. "Besides, we're done. And I honestly don't see myself with anyone else, male or female, for that matter."

"So you both just called it quits because you're afraid the team will find out?" he asks.

"Yeah," I answer.

"Was it more than just sex?"

"Huh?" I ask in confusion.

"Did you care about him, or was it just, you know, to get your rocks off?"

"I care about him," I admit, thinking how fucking strange it is to be talking about this with Quinton.

"You said that in the present tense," he points out.

"Yeah. And?"

"And that means you *still* care about him, not cared about in the past tense."

"So? I'm not ruining my career for..."

"For someone you care for, possibly even love? Why not, Lathan? I mean, I can see how it would be scary to drop that sort of bomb on everyone, but they can't boot you from the team for your sexual preference."

"I know that, but they can boot me from the team if we start playing like shit and it causes problems, making other teammates uncomfortable."

"Fuck them," Quinton says. "They can either support it, or they can go to another team."

"Right, I'm sure the coaches and owners would get right on board with that motto."

"Just think about it," he says. "I don't know how you feel about Pax; but if it were me, I wouldn't give a shit what anyone said. There's no way I would give up Callie for this team or anything else. I love her. She's my family now, and that's more important than football."

"So, you're not weirded out by it?" I ask him. "I mean, are we still friends?"

"What the fuck kind of question is that?" he snaps at me. "Just because I don't play for that particular team doesn't mean I have a problem with you on it. Honestly, I'm just glad you finally popped your cherry. *That* was something to be seriously concerned about," he teases with his signature crooked grin.

"Good, thanks," I tell him, amazed that my honesty didn't revolt him.

"Hey, guys," Roxy says when she wanders down the aisle and stops at our row. "Am I hearing things, or did one of you say Pax's name a few minutes ago?" she asks with a knowing smile directed right at me.

Fuck, she knows!

Did Pax tell her?

No, he wouldn't have, even if he was angry at me. Roxy must have figured it out seeing him at the funeral.

"Nope, I said packs, I needed some *packs* of peanuts," Quinton lies to Roxy, not the least bit convincing.

"Oh, well, either way, I wanted to see if you two would come with Kohen and me to *Moby Dick's*, Pax's club. It's opening this Friday night. Callie and Kelsey could come to, you know, to show your heterosexual support and get him some free press. He's freaking out, worried it's not gonna do well, and then he'll have to move back to Tennessee."

"*Moby Dick's*," Quinton repeats with a chuckle. "That's hilarious. And yeah, I'll check with Callie, but I'm sure she'll agree to come," Quinton agrees. "Oh, but we'll need Kelsey to babysit, so I guess you'll be going *stag* that night, Lathan."

Already shaking my head, I tell them, "No way. I can't go alone to a gay club. Everyone will think I'm gay."

"Fine," Quinton says. "I won't take Callie as my date. Will everyone think *I'm* gay?"

"Probably," I tell him with a bark of laughter.

"So, who cares?" he asks before he unbuckles his seatbelt and gets to his feet.

Oh, fuck me, this can't be good.

"Attention everyone!" Quinton yells loudly with his hands cupped around his mouth to get all our teammates to look at him. "I'm going to *Moby Dick's*, a new gay club that Roxy's friend is opening this Friday night. I'm not gay; but if I was, does anyone have a problem with that?"

My face burns like the desert sun at noon, so I duck my head behind the seat in front of me to hide it.

Several guys laugh, repeating the name again before a few deep voices mutter nos.

"I asked if anyone would have a problem with me being gay! So, as your team captain, I want everyone to answer me," Quinton repeats louder, more authoritative.

"*No, sir*!" a chorus of masculine voices along with Roxy's reply.

"That's what I thought, not that it's anyone's business," he says before he retakes his seat next to me.

"I'm gonna kill you," I warn him quietly through clenched teeth.

"But then you wouldn't be able to thank me after Friday night," he replies with a smug grin. "You're going, right? Or will Roxy and I have to drag you there?"

"And we'll do it too," Roxy says from the aisle.

"Fine, yes, I'll go. But that's it," I agree.

CHAPTER 34

Pax

"This place looks amazing!" Roxy says when she comes up to me right before the doors of *Moby Dick's* open to the public Friday night.

"Yeah, it does," I agree proudly as I glance around the immaculate living room that's been transformed into a dance floor underneath an enormous chandelier. The enclosed pool out back is sparkling green with red tiki torches surrounding it and festive lights hanging from the cabana. Upstairs, the bedroom walls were removed and the rooms renovated into one huge lounge area where you can still hear the music from the lower level but not quite as loud to make conversations easier.

"Now if I could just fill it with people," I tell her.

"I don't think that will be a problem," she says. "I've already seen a ton of *Moby Dick's* hashtags on Twitter and Facebook. People will come."

"We'll see," I reply. "I haven't done much paid advertising, just social media mostly because most people are busy getting ready for Christmas. I know it will take some time for the word to spread."

"The parking lot was full. Kohen had to drop me off to find a place," Roxy informs me with a broad smile.

"Full?" I repeat in disbelief. "That's sixty-two spaces. I thought that would be plenty. I mean, the maximum occupancy is two hundred, which seems low, I know, but I wanted memberships to be limited to up the exclusivity appeal."

Tonight and tomorrow we're open to the public with a flat cover charge for admission; but in order to come back, they have to buy a more expensive yearly membership.

"I think you're worried for nothing. This place is gonna do great, Pax," Roxy says, wrapping her arms around me for a hug. "Now, get back to work," she orders. "I'll find you later."

"See ya," I tell her as she wanders off.

I stand there in the middle of the empty room, gathering my wits and courage before I head over to my new employee that will be manning the check-in counter. Byron is a business student at the local university. And depending on how he does and his school schedule, I may even put him in charge on weekends.

"Is everything all set?" I ask him, tugging nervously on the sleeves of my suit.

"Yes, sir," he answers with a salute before he begins ticking off the list on his fingers. "Parking has become a slight problem, but Jay is directing overflow to the public parking lot three blocks away. The two bouncers are all set just outside the door with their security wands at the ready. The bars on the first and second floor are both fully stocked. Our lifeguard is sitting in his nest wearing a speedo that's hot enough to require mouth-to-mouth. So, whenever you're ready to open the doors, the DJ will cue up the music, and I've got plenty of wristbands and cash to make change." Byron holds up a wad of *Moby Dick's* bracelets and waves a hand toward his cash register like Vanna White.

"Great, that's...great," I tell him with a slap to his shoulder. "Then I guess it's time to get started."

Picking up his cell phone, Byron punches on the keys, and then upbeat music is filling the house.

"Nice," I tell him as I start for the front door. "Wish me luck."

"Good luck, Mr. Price," he calls out as I turn the knob and pull it open.

"Jesus Christ," I mutter when I see the line of people standing underneath the lamp posts and decorative lights, waiting to come inside.

"Ready, boss?" Jose, one of our bouncers, asks.

"Yep, start frisking and carding 'em," I tell him.

Turning back to Byron, I say, "If you need me, I have my phone on vibrate in my pocket. I'll just be hyperventilating into a brown bag up in my office."

"Got it," he replies with a wink.

"Don't forget the inside of the house maxes out at two hundred, so send them out to the pool if we go over," I remind him.

He rolls his eyes at me in the no-shit way. And since he appears to have everything under control, I jog up the stairs to make sure everything in the lounge and bar looks great before slipping into the one bedroom I turned into my office and close the door. There's not much in the space yet, just a wooden desk, rolling chair, laptop and file cabinet, but it's a nice place for me to hide and freak out in private.

Sitting down in the leather seat, I prop my feet up on the desk and try to calm down.

This is it. I did it. I opened my own club. While I don't imagine that this place will always be easy to run, I hope it does well and is worth the effort.

I know I should be downstairs celebrating right now, not sulking alone, but I just can't find the enthusiasm that I thought would come with my successful opening. In my fantasies over the last few weeks, I always pictured Lathan here dancing with me, even if it was just the two of us after hours. Celebrating tonight with Roxy is great, but it won't be the same.

...

Lathan

"I don't know about this," I say to Quinton as we wait in line on the street in front of *Moby Dick's*. Already tons of people, correction, tons of gay guys have come up to us and asked for autographs and selfies. No doubt, there are at least half a dozen posts on social media with one or both of us saying we're at a gay club.

"Dude, relax," he replies. "Your agent verified that, according to your contract, there's nothing the team or league can do about your sexual preferences. And if things don't work out with Pax, well, I'm pretty sure you have lots of other options around here."

"All of this seems like too much too fast," I grumble. "Shouldn't I start small? Tell my dad, Cameron and Nixon, and then work my way up to the entire public?"

"Okay, first of all, you said Pax slept with you in your childhood bedroom, so don't you think your dad probably solved that equation?" he asks.

"You think so?" I reply. "Maybe I should call him and warn him."

"Don't you want to see Pax first? I mean, if that doesn't work out, then this all gets swept under the rug as two heterosexual football players going to a club to support a friend, right?"

"Yeah, I guess," I mutter.

"And if I were you, I think just jumping in with both feet to get it over with would be better than slowly sticking one toe into the water at a time."

"That's easy for you to say; you're not the one coming out of the closet," I remind him.

"I'm trying to put myself in your shoes," he says. "You have to admit, getting it over with would be a huge relief, wouldn't it?"

"Yes," I reluctantly agree. "But that doesn't make it any less scary. Fans are gonna lose their shit, probably burn my jersey. The fallout is gonna be...awful."

"Don't think about the negative consequences. Think about the positive things that could come out of it. You could actually be happy for once," he argues. "Oh, and don't forget the most important aspect, you can get laid again."

Facepalming myself, I tell him, "Please stop. We're not going there again."

"Believe it or not, I've let a dude suck my dick before," Quinton informs me.

"Liar."

"I'm serious," he says, lowering his voice to a whisper. "It was my freshman year of college. I was drunk as fuck. He had long, blond hair, and I thought he was a chick."

"Really?" I ask in surprise.

"Yeah, crazy, right?" he answers. "Then, when it was over, I cupped the front of his jeans and bam! Hard dick."

"You're so full of shit," I tell him with a chuckle.

"Do you think I would make up a story like that? It happened, and you're the only person I've ever told. Not even Callie knows."

"So how was it?" I ask.

"Um, it was...you know, I don't really remember," he replies with a grin, telling me he's lying. That means he does remember and that it was good.

And now I know why he told me that story, to make me feel better about wanting to be with a man. Oddly enough, it worked. I don't feel as different and isolated from my best friend as I did before I told him about Pax and me. I couldn't have hoped for Quinton to have taken the news any better either, which has been a nice surprise. If you had asked me last week if the Wildcats star quarterback would ever be caught dead in a gay club, I would've said no fucking way.

Guess I was wrong, and I've never been so glad to be wrong.

"Here we go," Quinton says when we reach the front door next to the blue sign with the place's name and a fat white whale on it. Two big bouncers in all black start running metal detector wands over each of us, and then ask for our IDs.

Quinton pulls his out first, and the security guard does a double take at the license and up at Quinton.

"No shit!" the man exclaims.

"Yeah, that's me," Quinton replies.

The security guard nudges the other one who was scanning me. "Jose, look who these fuckers are!"

"I'll be damned," the other tall, thick man says. "Go on in, guys. Byron will take care of you."

Bryon will take care of us?

I can't help but wonder if Byron has been taking care of Pax ever since I last saw him weeks ago. If he has, it's my own damn fault.

Now I need to find him and talk to him.

"Hey, do you know where Pax is?" I ask the young guy sitting on a stool behind a podium when we get inside.

"I can check around. May I tell Mr. Price who's asking for him?" the man inquires with a brow raised.

Quinton jumps in and answers before I can. "A few of Roxy's friends from the Wilmington Wildcats."

"Nice! Wait just one second," the kid says before he picks up his cell phone and starts typing. "We're glad to have you, and I think you deserve the VIP treatment. Here are your bracelets. Go on in and help yourself to the bar. I'll let you know when I locate Mr. Price," he says, offering me and Quinton two navy blue leather bracelets that we take. There's a silver charm in the center with the shape of a fat whale cut out. It's...cute but still masculine.

"Thanks," I tell the guy before Quinton and I wander further inside. I have to admit that I didn't expect him to make it this far without chickening out.

The music grows louder as we approach the living room that's been turned into a large open dance floor with high ceilings. Several pairs of men are dancing, some even making out.

"Oh, look. There's a pool," Quinton says over the music, pointing toward the open doors at the back of the house.

"Let's go," I tell him since it looks less crowded out there. The outside is surrounded by a glass enclosure to keep it warm, so warm steam is rising from the pool.

"Too bad I forgot my speedo," Quinton jokes, nodding his head over towards the lifeguard. "Dude, don't look now," he leans over to whisper. "But some guys are checking us out."

My eyes flit quickly around the patio noticing *all* eyes are on us.

"No shit," I tell him. "What else did you expect when you decided to come here?" I ask.

"*Lathan*?"

I spin around at the sound of Pax's voice. Then I wish I had my phone out to take a picture of his surprised face, his body frozen in place with his hand on the knot of his silk tie. "Wh-what are you doing here?" he asks when he recovers, smoothing his hands down his tie as he approaches us.

"Pax! Congrats on the opening. This place is great," Quinton says, offering Pax his hand.

"Ah, yeah, thanks for coming, Quinton," Pax mumbles as they shake.

"Well, I think I need a drink," our quarterback says before he disappears back into the house.

"What are you doing here?" Pax asks me again.

"Apparently, I'm jumping in," I tell him, holding my arms out to my sides while dozens of eyes remain on us.

"Are you drunk?" he whispers.

"Nope, not yet. Maybe later, though," I reply honestly.

"No, seriously. What the hell are you thinking, Lathan?" he

snaps at me while making side-eyed glances around the room. "Someone could take a picture..."

"Pretty sure they already have," I tell him. "We did some selfies with fans out front while we were waiting."

"And what if...but aren't you worried..." he stammers, making me grin because Pax is always so composed and confident that it's funny to see him off balance because of me for once.

Without giving him a chance to recover, I step forward and reach for the back of his neck to kiss him. It's not just a quick peck either. I tongue fuck him like no one's watching, even though I know they are. And when Pax grabs my hips and pulls me closer, kissing me back, instead of worrying about who might find out and what they'll think about me being with a man, all I feel is...relief.

The truth is out.

Pax still wants me.

The rest we'll deal with together. Including what will probably be our first fight as a couple.

"Do you love me?" I ask against his lips.

"Yes," he answers with a smile.

"More than this suit?" I ask, gripping both sides of his collar.

Chuckling, he says, "Of course, baby," right before I kiss him again...then jump into the pool with him in my arms.

The water takes my breath away even though it's nice and warm. When my feet hit the bottom, I push myself up to the surface and make sure Pax is treading water instead of drowning. Turns out he can thankfully swim just fine. His head's already above the water, and he's sweeping his wet hair from his face.

"You fucker!" he yells as he laughs and pushes my head back under. "You owe me a new suit!" he says when I bob back up.

"Let's get that one off of you, and I'll start apologizing," I tell him, grabbing his collar to pull him over to the pool wall where I kiss him again.

"Deal," he agrees when he eventually pulls away. "Wanna see my office? It's not much yet, but it's private." His pride in this place is obvious and well deserved. I'm impressed by what he's accomplished on his own.

"Lead the way," I agree with a smile.

Pax leans on the edge of the pool to pull himself out of the water before offering me a hand that I take. Our soggy clothes that are now plastered to our bodies with puddles quickly forming at our feet.

Someone hands us both a towel that we use to wipe off our faces and dry our hair, but our outfits are lost causes.

"Come on," Pax says quickly making his way through the house and up the stairs. Thankfully, it's all hardwood floors or we would be making an even bigger mess.

As soon as he shuts the office door, we both start removing the wet clothes, forming a pile on the floor by the time we're both naked.

From across the room, the two of us stand there and admire each other's bodies for several long, silent moments before Pax says, "I still can't believe you're here."

"Believe it," I reply.

"There's no going back now," he tells me as he hops up and sits on the wooden desk behind him. "I mean, I guess you could try and say that you and Quinton were just here with friends and that your wife couldn't make it..."

"No, I'm not gonna lie anymore," I assure him as I step up between his thighs and reach for both sides of his face. "I know it won't be easy dealing with the media and angry fans, but to hell with them. You're worth it, because for the first time in my life you make me feel...alive, like there's finally a place where I belong."

"Ah, baby. I love you," Pax tells me. "I can't tell you how much it means that you're taking this risk for me."

"It's worth it. You're worth it," I assure him before I kiss him and show him just how much he means to me.

EPILOGUE

Pax

Ten months later...

Lathan has a way of making me do shit I would never do for anyone else.

Today is the first home game of the new football season, and I regret to admit that I'm wearing his navy blue and yellow, number eighty-six jersey with a pair of...*shudder*...jeans.

I figure dressing down and showing support for my man is the least I can do after he came out of the closet for me almost a year ago.

Surprisingly, not much was said by his fellow teammates, the league, or the fans after the big reveal. Maybe times are finally changing. I'm so damn proud of Lathan. Not a day goes by that he doesn't get an email or a letter from someone saying that he inspired them to be honest with themselves and come out to friends and family.

It was easy for me back in high school because I didn't have anything to lose other than my social standing. Lathan risked pretty much everything for me, and he didn't even hesitate once he made the decision. After the night of my club opening, he was all in. A few days later, he moved in with me, and we've been living our happily ever after since.

Moby Dick's is going strong, the popularity more than I could have ever imagined, which I figure I have Lathan and his team's publicity to thank for that. People from all over come to visit when they're on the east coast.

Life is great. There's nothing else I could possibly ask for. Well, except for one little thing that I refuse to rush Lathan into. He hasn't mentioned legally binding himself to me, and I haven't brought it up. While making Lathan mine officially would be awesome, I'm afraid he'll turn me down, so I haven't broached the subject even if I have thought about surprising him by popping the question.

"Pax," Roxy's dad says from the seat next to mine to get my attention after the players jog off the field for halftime.

"I'm gonna go grab a bite to eat," I tell him as I rise from my seat. "You need anything? How about you, Mr. Savage?" I ask Lathan's father, who is on the other side of me. He's been completely accepting of Lathan and me from the first day, which has been great. I know how important he is to Lathan after losing his mother, so I'm really glad he approves.

"Pax!" Mr. Benson says grabbing my shoulder and spinning me around to face the field again.

"What?" I ask him. "I want to hurry up and get back before the second half starts."

"Just hold your horses, Pax, and look across the stadium," Mr. Savage insists.

With a sigh of defeat, I finally lift my eyes to the section opposite ours.

"What is it?" I ask as I see the fans on the other side holding up the pieces of letters to spell something out. "Go, fight, win? Yeah, I've seen it all before. I'll be right back."

Grabbing the back of my neck, Mr. Benson turns me to the far left and says, "Read the whole thing for chrissakes!"

And that's when I finally read aloud what the entire half of the stadium is spelling out in all the little signs.

"*Will you marry me, Pax*? Holy shit! That's me. I'm Pax!" I exclaim in shock. "Wait. Do you think there's another Pax?" I ask Mr. Benson and Lathan's dad.

"You're the only Pax I know in this stadium."

Hearing Lathan's voice from the aisle, I spin around and find him standing there on the other side of his father, still in his grass-stained uniform except for the helmet. My jaw is practically on the cement. "What are you...you're supposed to be...is that..."

"You're speechless. That's a first, right?" Lathan asks with a grin before he reaches up to swipe the sweaty hair out of his red face. "Hey, Dad," he says to his father who stands up and gives him a quick hug.

"Good luck," Mr. Savage says before he moves past Lathan in the aisle so that he can get closer to me.

"I don't have much time, so I have to make this quick." Going down to one knee, Lathan holds up a silver ring with small diamonds embedded around the center of the thick band. "Paxton Price, for years I knew I was waiting for something great, someone incredible to come into my life. I just didn't know who. And then I met you, and you exceeded every expectation I had in the best possible way. You took the lead in convincing me to take a chance on loving you, so I thought it was time for me to step up and ask if you'll take a chance on marrying me."

I nod my answer until I can clear my throat to say it. "Yes. And damn you for making my eyes leak in public!"

"Mine are too," Lathan admits with a smile as he gets to his feet.

Reaching for my hand, he slips the ring onto my finger and then kisses it before he brings his lips to mine, right there in front of hundreds of thousands of people thanks to the camera broadcasting us on the jumbotron.

Lathan doesn't seem the least bit concerned about them and neither am I. So, I kiss my fiancé like he deserves to be kissed, without any hesitation and with an infinite amount of love.

The End

ALSO BY LANE HART

Thank you so much for reading Delay of Game!

Find out if Kelsey will get her own HEA in the next book in this series, Eligible Recievers.

When a newly single girl like me decides to play the field, what's better than one big, sexy, rough-and-tumble professional football player?

How about two of them?

Cameron and Nixon have been best friends for years, and now I've found myself in the middle of them.

Literally.

The two cocky wide receivers compete over everything – who kisses me better, who can last longer, who has the biggest...well, you get the point.

At first, it's all fun and games, until I start to fall for both of them. Hard.

But I'm just not the type of girl who sleeps with two men at the same time.

I would rather walk away from both rather than end up hurting one of them.

The problem is, I'm pretty sure that decision is out of my hands.

ABOUT THE AUTHOR

New York Times bestselling author Lane Hart was born and raised in North Carolina. She continues to live in the south with her husband, two daughters, and several pets named after *Star Wars* characters.

When Lane's not writing or reading sexy novels, she can be found in the summer on the beaches of the east coast, and in the fall watching football, cheering on the Carolina Panthers.

Join Lane's Facebook group to read books before they're released, help choose covers, character names, and titles of books! https://www.facebook.com/groups/bookboyfriendswanted/

Connect with Lane:

Twitter: https://twitter.com/WritingfromHart

Facebook: http://www.facebook.com/lanehartbooks

Instagram: https://www.instagram.com/authorlanehart/

Website: http://www.lanehartbooks.com

Email: lane.hart@hotmail.com

Made in United States
North Haven, CT
08 October 2025

80584468R00137